I0730862

THE SINGH SAGA

A Mountain Tale

Trophy D'Souza

WORKBOOK PRESS LLC
187 E Warm Springs Rd,
Suite B285, Las Vegas, NV 89119, USA

Website: https://workbookpress.com/
Hotline: 1-888-818-4856
Email: admin@workbookpress.com

Ordering Information:
Quantity sales. Special discounts are available on quantity purchases by corporations, associations, and others. For details, contact the publisher at the address above.

ISBN-13:   978-1-956017-17-5 (Paperback Version)
             978-1-956017-18-2 (Digital Version)

REV. DATE: 31.07.2021

DEDICATION

*This book
is dedicated to
my parents
who brought us up
-brothers & sisters-
to appreciate genuine values
and guided us
to keep united as
a family*

DISCLAIMER

*The book is a work of Fiction:
the possibility of characters or situations
being associated with people or places
today is purely accidental. References
made to individuals or to systems do not
intentionally depreciate people or values.
The motivational message of striving to
preserve family cohesion is
the underlying thought.*

ACKNOWLEDGEMENTS

- Particular thanks to WORKBOOK PRESS and its Management and Staff for taking the initiative and interest to re-publish the book so that it can be brought to a wider audience.

- A word of thanks to the Author House Publishing Team for all the help given to get this second book of mine published for the first time.

- Thanks especially to two close friends (who do not wish to be quoted beyond their initials – SAT & NAT) whose inspiration and encouragement helped with the development of this book.

- *Thanks also to many others who helped in the production of this book in different ways, including editing and proofreading, especially: Prem Kishore (USA), Phil Matthews (India), Joe Thompson (East Africa), CMPaul (India), Anu Mishra (USA), Fred Gomes (Australia), Jerry & Bernie Crasto (Canada), Beena Menon (India), Xavier Pinto (Canada).

Readers' Guidance: **Glossary & Map**

*The Glossary at the back of the book serves as a Guide to Readers who might need help with understanding the story and the themes presented.
*The interpretations in the Glossary have explained the way the Author sees the allusions.
*The words and phrases that might need explaining are 'referenced' with the ® symbol.
*The map of the Darjeeling Area should help in locating places mentioned in the book.
*The Author uses British English in general, but allows for some spelling in American English.

FOREWORD

The story is certainly an interesting analysis of how human relationships can be played out in society. The seamy side of each individual has been presented with startling frankness, with a wealth of controlled detail and appropriate language. The deep insights in the book show to what lengths the relationship between a man and a woman can go when unbridled passion rules over good sense.

The style in which the book is written makes it a believable account of life in the Himalayan hills. The spontaneity and vividness of the narrative keeps the reader totally engaged, although at times the geographical references would seem to interrupt the flow. However the various allusions and the magnificent descriptions, especially of the picturesque scenes in the Himalayas are quite poetic.

The characters are real and believable and come alive as the story progresses. The protagonists - Billu and particularly Sudha - take control over their own destinies, unaware that they are heading inexorably towards a downward spiral. Sadly inevitability rules the day, quite the way AC Bradley® analyses tragedy, where the tragic heroine and hero are not assured their 'promised land'®.

The book, with a very powerful beginning ends suitably in the Epilogue with the very lofty themes of forgiveness and reconciliation. In short, the book is a condensed file of the life of an average family in the hills with all its enthusiasm and disillusionment, and finally, fulfillment. The story is truly a Saga of the Singh family in the Himalayas.

Fred Gomes   *-Language Consultant, Queensland, Australia*

Reviewers' Comments

The book has an interesting flow, and the Himalayan ambience comes alive through the descriptions of the settings and the lives of the traders with their typical nomadic existence and travelling between towns and lodges. The relationships and liaisons that develop and the casualness or fickleness of the situations or otherwise add flavour to the way of life described in the book. Though there are a large number of characters involved the clever explanations and the lucid language make the tale an exciting read. The descriptions also skilfully describe involved scenes in language that is controlled yet imaginative.

Beena Menon   *Training Consultant: Teacher Education – British Council, India.*

The strong opening of the book sets the scene for a novel that is truly a powerful development of the two main characters, which makes the book a wonderful read. The characters are well described without the romantic episodes in any way dominating the overall portrayal of the plot. The geographical settings and the situations are explained in language that is both appropriate and absorbing. The drama and the suspense, especially at the beginning, make the reader eager to read on.

Xavier Pinto   *Consultant: Hospitality & Tourism Services, Toronto, Canada*

This interesting tale gives a glimpse of the type of life lived in the Himalayan hills. The central character in spite of her clever insinuations still seems to evoke sympathy because of the peculiar circumstances that surround her. The situations the book portrays probably arise out the pressured circumstances in which these people live out their lives. The underlying message in the Epilogue is powerful because, perhaps contrary to what some people might believe, it is the vibrancy and broad-mindedness of the younger generation that bring sense to the Saga.

Joe Thompson   *Consultant: Youth Ministries, East Africa*

The author has done an excellent exposure of characters who would have been 'lost in the woods' otherwise. In fact, in spite of the unpleasantness of some situations, the story offers a wonderful portrayal of life in the mountains and the stresses and strains that people go through both in family life as well as in the actual difficulties of everyday living. The themes presented too, especially in the Epilogue, are uplifting, not to speak of the encouraging way in which a younger generation faces the future. The book is an absorbing read also because of the way the language keeps the reader interested.

Bernie & Jerry Crasto   *Community Officers, London - Ontario, Canada*

People live their lives conditioned by the circumstances around them. The characters in the book are no different. The author has carefully portrayed the settings of life in the hills quite the way it is, in quite a balanced way so that the readers can make their own judgments. Once again patience and good sense come through in the end, and young people offer hope and optimism as people who can uphold the values that make for a good society: reconciliation and optimism. The book is worth a read.

Phil Mathews   *Consultant: Youth Ministries, North India*

THE AUTHOR

Trophy D'Souza, who has first-hand experience of dealing with people in different situations in life, analyses how family values can easily be eroded from within in his second book, The Singh Saga. His first book, A Bumpy Ride, which also deals with people, shows how dysfunctional managers can affect people's lives in organizations.

He brings to his books a wealth of experience as a teacher, youth worker, manager and education advisor in Asia and Europe, and in Africa too where he also set up voluntary social-education projects. Now based in the UK, he teaches English Language courses, conducts ESL projects and writes life stories, and occasionally contributes to sports, music and news blogs. He also promotes Quantified Assessments he designed, which were used in two colleges in the UK and two in India.

Trophy brings to his writing his captivating style of language, packed with humor, wit and information, which also reflects his interests in drama, music, history and literature, and his travel experiences in different countries.

THE SINGH SAGA

A Mountain Tale

CONTENTS

THE SINGH SAGA
A Mountain Tale

Chapter 1
The setting sun

Just as the sun was setting in this idyllic mountain resort in the Himalayas ®, Billu had just managed to sneak in by the side stairs unnoticed by the bouncers and had met up with his tryst. He had hurried up the narrow flight of stairs to that corner of the terrace, half-hidden by the water tank rushing into the arms of his beloved Sudha. This was the third time he had managed to hold her close, in clandestine settings unknown to his wife of 17 years, Chula, and unnoticed by any gossipers in a locked embrace that meant so much to them. No words were spoken.

This time however, there was an unwelcome and disturbing surprise. No sooner had Sudha collapsed into Billu's strong supporting manly arms than there was a loud, rasp-like screech.

"Stop it, Billu…Stop it…There you are… I knew it….. Stop it….," came the shrill yell from Chula, as painful as it was disturbing, resembling the frustrating screams of a partner seeing a lover about to fall off a cliff.

Recovering quickly from her paramour's binding hold and quick to react Sudha responded with a violent blast of teenage passion.

"You can't do anything... I'll take your husband away from you... I will."

Choking with embarrassment at being discovered and with no plausible explanation, Billu attempted to reply in muttering confusion.

"It's .... It's ....not... what you think."

In a flood of tears rolling down her cheeks, flushed with anger and in wild desperation, Chula just couldn't help but blurt out.

"I knew this all along." She paused briefly for breath and then screamed again with tears flowing down her flushed cheeks, "Stop it...You can still stop it...She only wants your money...You will never love her....she's only a teenager." She paused again still gasping for breath. "We've loved each other so many years....we have our children ...to bind us together." She stopped once more and went into a spurt of angry crying and then continued, "She has given you nothing...She will finish you."

Like a wounded tigress fighting off her rival, Sudha came back even stronger, re-enkindled by her powerful teenage zest.

"I've told you already....and I'll say it again...I love him madly." She then continued with arrogant determination, "You don't have a hope in hell....He is now my beloved....I love him...you don't....Just keep off."

"Can't you say something?" pleaded a wounded Chula, still gasping for breath hoping in desperation that Billu would come to his senses.

Gripping Billu even more passionately and throwing down the gauntlet in a flaunting challenge, Sudha seemed to have had the last word.

"Just leave us alone....and move on."

The sun had set that day, but not for Sudha. That discovery did not in any way cool off the wild passion of these lovers. Chula had been just about able to drag herself home that night, crestfallen but not defeated. She had played the good wife to Billu and had weathered nearly seventeen years of marriage and had given Billu three lovely daughters: Laila, Saima and Bindya. She was naïve to believe that she still had a hold on Billu.

It was during her post-natal recovery after Bindya's birth, when Chula was weak and not quite available to Billu's affections that Sudha had latched on to him. Billu was in more ways than one vulnerable and lonely, as he had to travel out for weeks at a stretch to attend to the government projects he was managing in the valleys around.

During that period Billu had wandered into this resort pub in Soonadah®, in the Himalayan hills not far from his flat to share his frustrations with some of his mates. When the last of them had left there came along this 16-year-old girl, Sudha, swaying and swishing about daintily to serve the guests in the late evening session. That evening the lady owner, Saara, had also left the keys of the pub with her to lock up at the end of the night as she had to rush off on some personal business. She trusted Sudha with that important chore as she knew that Sudha whom she had grown fond of lived with a friend just opposite the resort. It wasn't the first time that Saara had entrusted her with that responsible task.

Sudha, though that evening had other ideas. Her ever-active brain, which was always looking for opportunities had devised a secret plan. She had set her eyes on Billu for quite some time and had kept a close watch on his movements. She noticed that he was lonely and on that evening had picked up part of a conversation when Billu had shared with his mates some of his frustrating situations at work and of a few of his boring chores at home. Sudha had the eyes of a hawk focused on her prey, with her teenage passion aroused like a tigress in heat. There was no stopping her. The orphan, starved for love and caring for so many years, felt this was an occasion not to be missed.

Nearly a year had passed since she had had that memorable liaison with Gonkul, the Sikkimese® trader who had brought her there. That virgin night of passion with him in that same resort in Soonadah had nearly faded away, but it had shown her that she could get what she wanted. Gonkul at that moment seemed like a distant past with Billu like a fresh offerings on a silver platter. She felt she was in the driving-seat and had to act quickly. Her instincts seemed to drive her on.

When all the other customers had left, she found a way to shut the main door and then to move towards Billu who now nearly inebriated with the local brew, had also drunk in that sexy concoction of beautiful locks and dilating eyes as Sudha came and sat opposite him. He had noticed her on previous occasions, but that night when everything seemed doomed and gloom to him she was like a heaven-sent angel. His eyes, though droopy has been yet lazily surveying that soothing female presence smiling charmingly across the table. Their eyes met and she noticed he was succumbing to her powerful desires. She then glided in, seductively closer to him and was soon sitting right next to him.

Billu relished the tender attention he was getting, something he so sorely missed. He let her run her fingers gently through his bushy hair as he slowly sunk into her arms. Sudha herself couldn't believe that she had enticed her prey so easily and so successfully. The pursuing tigress, quite contrary to animal behavior patterns, had overpowered the tiger completely, covering him with her flowing tresses.

"Now, you don't need to worry.....," she began. "You are safe with me," she assured him. "You need love: you will get it...plenty of it... trust me...You need it.... Just come here when you need to relax. Just be yourself." She then continued whispering into his ear soothingly, "Stay close...and don't worry...I'm here for you...come when you need comfort.....I'm always here...."

As she held him close he felt soothed and comforted as though a heavenly being had gently cast a spell over him. Once he was in her grasp, she took over. She then led him to a couch nearby, and was soon in control as they were locked in each other's arms. It seemed for the couple that the night would never end with Sudha the more aware that she had made a successful move. She was elated that she had played her cards right. It seemed like a night's taking had turned gold. Sudha felt she had her precious prey thoroughly sedated and under control in her grasp. She was a little worried that she would not be able to meet up so easily in public and suggested to Billu that they meet at particular times on that terrace.

Meeting up at any convenient point was alright for Billu, but he still couldn't get himself to accept that he had fallen head over heels for his highland lass® who was not even half his age. He couldn't believe his luck that just out of nowhere, only about 200 yards away from his rented room, a soft-spoken female companion would be cheering him up after so many apparently frustrating years with a partner who for him was not satisfying his desires anymore.

Chula now in her forties, was full of apparently genuine conjugal love, but not of the vitality or the passion she had originally shared with a fiery Billu, who always seemed to be searching for new experiences of love. Just when Billu thought his world was sinking, he found his rescue ship, his lighthouse of direction, his nymph® of satisfaction. That seemed to have been the longest night of his life, a night he wished would never end, one of hours of passion, where he felt he had re-discovered what he thought was love.

For Sudha, the fair-skinned pretty teenager, the catch was not just the meeting of all her desires of love and passion, but one with an older man dark-skinned yet brawny though more than twice her age. Age or skin tone didn't really matter or perhaps it did as the trend with her buddies was to pursue older partners somewhat seasoned since they purported to offer more satisfaction as well as more security and stability than dashing brash teenagers. Moreover she felt convinced that beauty was what she saw, and Billu ticked all the boxes at least in her manhunt list.

Billu to his buddies and to his female admirers, was the quiet achiever who did his work and then chilled out in the quiet respectable company at the end of the day. In any case he wasn't with his family in the evenings and he needed his mates or perhaps a mate to share some of his experiences or maybe his frustrations. Work often took him to different distant places that left him tired, but this friendly lodge seemed like an ideal place, where no one really bothered to check on who he really was. He too felt he could relax here, and the sweetness and kindness of Sudha, especially for that evening seemed to relieve some of his inner hang-ups that he could not really share with his mates. Each time he got to the lodge he seemed to grow fonder of her.

However, there was a past to Billu too, one that he hadn't even revealed to Chula, his wife. He had taken his chances with women, usually older females, generally at lodges or at private homes and they had kept his secrets. Billu, in other words knew how to play his cards right. He also knew that Chula, fortunately, was not a jealous wife and that she would never probe his dark secrets. What Billu was not aware of was that Sudha was not a fresh chicken. She had earlier fallen temporarily at least for her knight in a shining land-rover, Gonkul, the trader who had rescued her from a somewhat uncertain future in Sikkim® just about a year earlier. That too was a near-spontaneous link up with an older man, in this very same resort, in the hope of a relationship.

For Sudha, was it love now with Billu? Was it a genuine start to a permanent relationship? Or was it the end of the clever and persistent search of an orphan who hadn't really experienced true love and care?

In Sikkim® Sudha had experienced the care and kindness of some neighbors and had also been exposed to some others, hard task masters, who had taken advantage of her beauty and inexperience to exploit her for slavish poorly-paid work. As a daughter of a local laundry man, a dhobi[®], she was unfortunate to have lost her father when she was hardly 10. Her mother brought her up and gradually got her to help in the laundry trade. She grew up to be quite an endowed teenager with her beauty attracting the attention both of teenagers and of young men.

Sudha, forced by circumstances to take on a more adult role, was quite naïve in the beginning. She thought that she could fight her own battles, almost taking over her dad's place while trying to groom her younger brother, 4 years junior, to take on the man's role in the family. Just when she thought she could face up to everything she nearly lost her virginity when she was hardly 15, almost trapped by one of those silly teenage bashes that often ruins budding ambitions. A strange mix of bravado and posturing had helped to keep her above board.

Gonkul, the Sikkimese trader had noticed Sudha as she grew up. He had laundered his clothes with her dad and then had passed by their little place on numerous occasions, even after her dad had passed away. He had observed her go through her mundane chores and had thought that she could really have risen above her station and have achieved more in life. He also noticed the bunch of surly men, adults and teenagers, who were hovering around like vultures ready to pounce on this teenage beauty. He gradually broached the subject with her mother of taking her away on one of his trips to find her better employment. He knew he had to do it without cutting off the support she gave to her family. Gonkul, who was single treated Sudha's family almost like family and was often hopping by for a cup of tea and a brief chat. In some ways he was their newspaper, their link person, their friend and their advisor when they needed help. This time he was offering help and advice that showed his genuine concern.

Gonkul, who was known around as a benevolent and considerate person, a sort of 'good' trader and who was believed for his views, his advice and his influence, finally got Sudha's mother to let her go when the next trip came up. Quite fortunately, her brother was gradually taking over her chores and so her mother felt assured that she could let her daughter go.

Sudha, who had somehow survived those playful nights at local pubs and teenage bashes without blemish, had not really learnt her lessons. She had developed manipulative ways that almost blinded her to the fact that as a growing woman she was vulnerable. Yet her instinctive caution had kept her unscathed except for Gonkul and now Billu, who seemed to meet up to some of her aspirations and ambitions. She felt uncertain in a sense, but she also felt that her womanliness was affecting her determination and resolve. At some moments she felt lonely and weak at others, she felt as strong as steel. The real Sudha enigma was unraveling.

Chapter 2

The Rising Moon

Indeed, some crumbs of fortune did come her way when Sudha was able to tag on to this wandering merchant, Gonkul a year earlier. Gonkul was a Sikkimese trader who had business links with several traders on this trade route from Sikkim to Siliguri®. Sikkim, an independent state in India, is somewhat cut off from more developed trading centres in the country and so there was scope for enterprising traders to establish business links with other towns.

Sikkim's capital Gangtok®, is where Gonkul's parents and grandparents had set up business. They were of Nepali origin and descended from ancestors who had natural business skills that were honed by years of dealings with traders from Nepal®, China, India and Bhutan®, countries which bordered Sikkim. They dealt with perfumes, spices, woolen garments, and even smaller household goods including electronic items like cookers, irons, shavers and hair dryers. If Sikkim was close to a few countries, Siliguri, at the bottleneck of north Bengal, was also an excellent trading link to some bordering Indian states: Bihar in the west and Assam not too far away in the east. On the east as well was another country, Bangladesh®. Indeed, there were a lot of possibilities for trade for Gonkul and other traders.

Gonkul had developed good speaking and negotiating skills. He had been to college in Darjeeling® and could speak fluent Nepali, Hindi® and English of course and had also picked up some conversational exchanges in Bengali®. During his college days at Saint Joseph's College, Darjeeling, he had made friends with students from other parts of the region, who later developed their own businesses. One of these student-friends, now turned trader was Pandu in Sikkim and the other were Sanjuk in Siliguri who ran a clothing manufacturing business.

Once on returning from one of his trips he was pleasantly surprised to find that Sudha had moved away from her dhobi chores and had begun working strangely enough for his trading partner, Pandu. He was indeed glad to see her there in a way pleased for her that she had moved on. Yet he felt she was capable of better things. He thought Sudha was too attractive and efficient for the menial jobs she was doing at Pandu's place. He seemed to notice that she was slaving away as a domestic attendant when he thought she really had more skills to offer. Pandu, his ex-college friend who now shared business deals with him lived close to Gonkul's apartment, in Gangtok®. He also had a little resort for travelers which Gonkul frequented for business chats and for local gossip.

Gonkul while chatting away on this occasion sipping the local brew together and sharing friendly talk about things business and otherwise thought he might share an idea or two with Pandu about Sudha. He suggested to Pandu his intention of taking Sudha with him on the trip he was planning, to Siliguri. He believed that Pandu wasn't possibly giving Sudha a fair chance to express her self or to develop her real potential. He had got this impression of her while having a brief chat with Sudha as she served him food and drinks.

Sudha worked during the day with Pandu doing his chores at home and then spent the evenings as a waitress in his resort. Pandu too didn't have a family. He only had his ageing parents to look after. He too lived a lot like Gonkul, travelling frequently to do trade and getting back to base to check on his parents and on his local business. He had a manager who looked after his interests at his resort when he was away and he got Sudha to check on his parents at home.

Pandu's parents were after him to settle down but he kept putting it off as he found the excitement of his female contacts in the villages and towns where he did business a lot more interesting than married life as he saw it. He felt that these liaisons were just about adequate to help him balance his business and his personal life, quite like a lot of his business mates. In the year or so that Sudha had got used to her chores with him he hadn't made any approaches to her. While Sudha too hadn't crossed any boundaries in her relationships, Gonkul always showed her a measure of tenderness and caring.

"You know I was thinking about your girl who helps you, I mean Sudha," Gonkul broke into the conversation with Pandu that bordered on girls and affairs, and maids and masters anyway.

"What about her?" Pandu questioned, almost alerted to protect himself about something quite personal. He was afraid that Gonkul might be a little intrusive about his trying it on with Sudha.

"No, I don't mean anything suspicious in any way," Gonkul was quick to ward off any suggestion of Pandu's personal interest in the teenage beauty which it was reasonably safe to assume might have been the case.

"So? What about Sudha?" asked Pandu, his voice almost quivering through the intoxicating fumes of the 'hookah'® he was inhaling.

"I want to try and get her into some employment that will help her on in life," Gonkul explained.

"You mean I'm treating her badly?"

"No, not at all…It's just a suggestion and I know you are a kind man and treat people well. Moreover, I've known you for years and know how kind and considerate you are. But this is different," Gonkul elaborated.

"So, what do you have in mind?" Pandu hesitated to ask.

Gonkul, who had a soft side, took pity on Sudha and was able to make an arrangement with Pandu, who was quite close to him as one of his trading partners in Sikkim. He worked out a deal, a sort of temporary payout and took Sudha in his caravan land-rover on a five-hour ride from Sikkim to Kalimpong® and then on to Ghum® bypassing Darjeeling® nearby to move on to this little mist-locked one-horse town, Soonadah. Here he hoped to make a stopover for a night in a resort that he had often visited before he then moved on to Siliguri in the plains, via Kurseong®.

Gonkul had really planned to take Sudha all the way down to the plains of Siliguri as he had explained to Pandu. He hoped his other merchant friend, Sanjuk, who employed girls in his sewing industry there would offer her some meaningful employment. He thought that this change of scene would start her off and that she could then get on in life. On his return Gonkul promised Pandu that he would get him another girl to do his chores. In fact Gonkul went further and gave Pandu a maid from one of his other business contacts to fill in the gap during Sudha's absence until the new permanent replacement arrived.

However Saara, the resort owner where Gonkul stopped over took a liking to Sudha both for the way she came across and for the orphan background she came from. Moreover both Gonkul and Sudha thought the offer of a waiter's job was too good to refuse. There was no interview and there were no questions asked. Sudha didn't require a CV and Saara needed no references. It was quite near love at first sight, where a job was concerned. Saara herself had lost her husband through an unfortunate road accident. She had adopted a boy and a girl earlier, orphans, who were under the care of nuns[®] in a convent[®] in Kalimpong. Saara knew one of the nuns quite well and was able to iron out her suitability as a parent. The two children had grown up to become responsible adults in society. Beside the fact that Saraa knew how to look after and bring up orphans, she also took a fancy to Sudha, to her beauty and to her pleasant manners and told Gonkul what she thought.

"I quite like Sudha," Saara told Gonkul the next morning after he was up from a refreshing night's sleep.

"Yes, she's not just a pretty girl. She's quite capable," Gonkul agreed.

"That's exactly what I want to say....You think you could leave her with me? I think I know how to look after orphans. I'm sure I can care for her and teach her a few things. She could well be a very good waitress and a helper in many other ways too. She looks very capable to me. What do you think?"

Gonkul hadn't expected that, as it meant a change of plans for him. But he had good sense enough to see the point of an experienced guardian for Sudha as well as a safe haven for her with meaningful employment too, at least for a time. Though Saara knew how to cope with bringing up orphans, in the case of Sudha she took a risky leap into the unknown, totally unaware of who Sudha really was. She would have to trust Gonkul's word. She seemed prepared to do that as she and Gonkul were quite close and he was quite her confidant.

"I can see the point...Though I think I told you I'd really wanted to take her down to Siliguri and get her to learn a trade and so then become self-sufficient...But this experience with you training her is also a good option, at least for the time being. Maybe Siliguri can wait," Gonkul agreed.

Sudha too wasn't sure of her future and had got used to the kind and trusting ways of Gonkul though she had known him for only a short time, actually only during this rather long and tedious five-hour land-rover ride and of course the hours he had spoken to her at the resort. Perhaps it was the confidence that Gonkul inspired, that made Sudha realize that it was in her best interests to take up this job, at least temporarily.

Sudha felt deeply indebted to Gonkul for all the interest he was taking in her welfare and so late that night, before Gonkul went off the next morning, she thought she would meet up with him to thank him for all his kindness. There was quite a long chat in his little room, with him quaffing down his beer and with her listening to tales of his frequent travels. As the tale-telling continued she found herself getting closer to him, emotionally especially and physically too. As she kept pouring in the beer she also continued to tell Gonkul more of her own sad past. Gonkul hadn't heard all that before and kindhearted as he was, he literally melted at her sob stories. He hadn't known much about her beyond her being the daughter of his friend the dhobi.

As the night grew weary for Gonkul, he also grew in pity and in admiration for Sudha who had suffered so much. Sudha felt drawn to his loving ways and was amazed at his many adventures, his business skills and his ability and experience to be able to handle different types of situations. As she moved forward for a last hug and then tried to put him into bed, she found herself hugging and kissing him. What she didn't expect, though she had secretly hoped for it, was that Gonkul's initial response, which seemed just platonic initially, soon developed into a near passionate hugging.

Gonkul did have the occasional fling and had linked up with Saara during one of his visits, one late winter night, when they had chatted late into the night, exchanging their stories of adventure.

Gonkul and Saara were about the same age and as they kept drinking the local brew they got closer and soon passion bonded them for the whole night. Saara who was lonely and unloved to a measure was thrilled at this unexpected experience while Gonkul felt grateful to her for awakening his tender side and for enkindling his dormant passions. Then too, on that occasion it was Saara who had led him on with her soothing feminine charms. All the same he felt that the affair with Saara was a one-off and Saara too had kept her distance on other visits and didn't mind if Gonkul brought along his own friends, male of female.

This time it was different with Sudha. As Sudha hugged him tightly he felt gently aroused and soon found he was responding with manly eagerness to a younger and fresher love than what Saara had offered earlier. The Saara affair looked like a distant past, almost a year since it had happened and Gonkul sensed a feeling of bonding as he responded to Sudha's powerful advances. He thought he had a sort of duty to protect her and so letting himself go seemed like he was being protective as well as re-enkindling his virile passion, which seemed to have lain dormant for quite a while. Sudha hadn't really planned this, but her youthful energy and excitement responded as they both relished each other's love and warmth in that locked embrace.

Sudha too had never really let herself go even during all those earlier teenage pranks, but here she felt drawn into Gonkul's loving arms that seemed to her to be as strong as they were caring. In that moment she forgot all about her precious virginity and about genuine love. This was wild passion and she just relished it. The hours passed and when daylight came, Sudha hurried back to her room before Saara would get any scent of what had gone on upstairs, in fact in the room just above hers on the ground floor. However, for the two of them it looked like this was an initial pact of love, an explosion that seemed to work towards a fusion, an engagement and a bond that both hoped would last. Gonkul was like a rising moon of light and hope for her. She felt she had made a conquest.

"Please stop by when you are going back...And come and see me. I will miss you so much," Sudha pleaded. "You have been so good to me...You treated me so well....and last night you were so wonderful...I felt your protection and love...you were so good.....I will be thinking of you," she said as tears of joy rolled down her lovely cheeks. "I need you so much. You must come back," she insisted.

Gonkul didn't really expect that she would have fallen for him. He had not intended it that way, as he had his paramours in other towns, those more of his age. They were the sort of traders' one-off trysts with lonely women who cared for them, offering them warm hospitality: food for the fare and a bed to share. It was a special relationship that the women too looked forward to. Gonkul never spoke about these discreet liaisons which he had at nearly all the major stops along the trade route.

But this encounter with Sudha's teenage vigor seemed to give him new energy and hope, something different that he had not experienced before. It was a night too satisfying to forget, even though she was so much younger than all the women he had met on his many travels. She was really only about half his age. But he had enjoyed her wild exuberance, her teenage passion and her adventurous love. This exciting link up with a beautifully endowed woman, fresh and ebullient, made him forget his mundane trading chores and seemingly quite elevated his horizons, feeling triumphant as though he had won the prize of a vestal® virgin after she had been released from her temple commitment.

Gonkul was handsome of a swarthy complexion, slightly more toned than most sturdy men and really charming. He wasn't much of a speaker when it came to tender words, but his feelings apparently were deep and powerful and the unction seeped through as he stammered.

"Yes, of course...I'll come....I will miss you... We will meet again.....for a long night." He then managed to fumble on, "and maybe, we can link up...for a long day, I mean a long life together...I feel that way...Do you want the same?"

"I too want that....very much," she sort of drooled. "You have become dear to me....Last night was amazing! You were really wonderful.... You're so good... You give me hope for the future!"

That last embrace in that night of passion had lasted longer than he had expected, but for Sudha it was her way of saying 'thank you'. It had taken only minutes for her powerful teenage feelings to take over and it all developed the way it was heading, into an intense night of ravishing love she would want to remember for a long time. She couldn't be too sure but she felt Gonkul was her answer: a trader with money, a man of passion and a person who cared. She felt safe with him and she sensed her confidence growing. Above all she thought she was feeling true love for the first time. She had this strange feeling of certainty that she was playing her cards right. So, was this going to be her future?

Meanwhile a tempting offer of a contract with a double deal came along for Billu and he had to decide to move away at least temporarily to this other small mountain town of Mirik® more than 40 km away from little lonely Soonadah. Billu had to take up a room in this distant hilly place to be close to his work with options of a weekly or bi-weekly visit back home to Chula and his three children, in Soonadah. But does distance really foster enchantment?

Hidden passions cannot be bridled and the flame lit on that dusky evening in the setting sun had left Sudha quite lonely and fairly depressed. In less than a fortnight she had found her way to Mirik. Soon the Soonadah gossip recorded that Sudha had disappeared while Chula's Wikileaks® had given her all the cues she was looking for. She got the leads and decided to track down her husband. Once again, one late evening after the sun had set she crash-landed near the little motel room where she found the paramours locked unabashedly in love. She was staring shocked and horrified at a scene that spoke more conclusively than what she had seen and heard on that fateful night on the resort terrace in Soonadah.

This time Billu was not just visibly shaken. His reaction switched dramatically from the passion of love to that of wild fury. He looked more like a wounded tiger disturbed in his lair and nearly stretched for a left jab at Chula. It was evident there was no attachment anymore to their wedding promises nor to any loyalty even to his children. Chula survived the night in a tiny motel nearby, while Billu desperately, in quite a confused frame of mind, planned speedy divorce proceedings.

Chapter 3
Growing Roots

Billu's parents, Ratan and Chandni had moved into the hills in the 1960s when Ratan had received an offer from the Darjeeling Forest Department to be an officer in the Darjeeling outpost close to Ghum, a little town only about 5 km before Darjeeling on the Siliguri-Darjeeling road link. Billu's father, Ratan Singh originally from Bihar, had worked in the forest areas of Assam® in north east India, but had married a girl from Nepal®, Chandni, the daughter of one of his work associates there whose family had relatives in Kurseong. They had met at a college in Patna®, in Bihar®, where Chandni's father had sent her for business studies. The relationship had lasted the distance both in space and in time with just the occasional telephone call helping in the bonding process, quite a feat in those days of no mobile phones and no internet.

Ratan's association with his wife's relatives and with his work compelled him to look for a home in Ghum, in the Darjeeling area closer to Chandni's folks, who lived not far away in Kurseong about 25 km away. Ghum, which has one of the highest points of any railway in the world and is the highest railway station in India, is the next little town after Soonadah on the Siliguri to Kurseong-Darjeeling road and narrow-gauge rail route. Ghum has two important tourist attractions: the Ghum Buddhist Monastery, mentioned in travel and mystery books and Tiger Hill, one of the best viewing points in the world for a breathtaking sunrise. Ghum is also a junction for road routes to Kalimpong in the east and Mirik® on the south west, two other little towns in the Darjeeling area.

Ghum, at 2225 meters proved too cold, wet and misty for Ratan's family and he decided to move to Kurseong, nearly 1000 meters lower than Ghoom, where he eventually built what he thought would become the family's base. He built his dream home about 100 metres away from the Kurseong railway station. It was just about 50 metres above the railway tracks that ran alongside the only tarred road, the famous Hill-Cart Road that linked Darjeeling near the Himalayas to the lush tea-gardens and plains of Siliguri.

The choice of Kurseong for a home was not an easy decision as it was quite a distance away from his work in the Ghum area. It really meant that Ratan would be away for most of the week unless of course he chose to travel daily. He tried both options. He began by commuting but soon found it too taxing and settled for renting a room in the Ghum area close to his work. He came home some weekends and often made those weekends longer just to be able to spend more time with his 6 children who were growing up.

There was a constant flow of landrover-taxis plying the route between Ghum and Kurseong and it didn't really take more than an hour each way. Ratan knew that the options were there whenever he needed to travel and even though it was a distance from Ghum, Kurseong would be, he thought a better place to set up home and bring up his children. That's exactly what he did and brought up his three sons -Biru, Shidu and Billu- and his three daughters -Brinda, Deena and Lynda- there, making use also of the education facilities in Kurseong.

Biru Singh, Ratan's eldest son showed no inclination towards taking up forestry and decided to train to be a teacher. He soon married Balti, a junior school teacher who was quite a beauty and they were able to start off a little primary school in the Kurseong area. The school ran well initially and even grew to a Standard 3 level taking in Kindergarten children as well. However neither Biru nor Balti had a financial bent and they were soon in debt after only a year.

Meanwhile, Shidu Ratan's second son was able after his high school studies to migrate to Canada on a business plan, recruited on the regular immigration points-plan as he had done an extended course in

Accountancy in his B.Com degree. It worked for him, and soon he was able to send financial help to his elder brother, Biru, to continue exploring the school option. In fact, it enabled Biru and Balti to shift their school project in the plains area of Siliguri. That too folded up after another two years. At that point, help came also from another source for the couple.

Brinda had gone to Bangalore in South India to train as a nurse. She was really the next child after Biru, in pecking order, and had financial help from both her father, Ratan, as well as later, some support from her younger brother, Shidu, to complete her nursing-school training. Brinda was fortunate to get a placement in a private Kalimpong hospital, almost immediately after she had finished her training. A year later she got recruited for work in a government hospital in Oman, in the Middle East, and earned and saved up, over nearly two decades, so that she could also help some members of the family. She did step in to rescue Biru and Balti, besides building her own house in the plains of Siliguri.

Deena, on the other hand was not as fortunate as Brinda. She stayed at home, after high school, to look after her ageing mother and father, Chandni and Ratan. In that rather busy yet monotonous role of home-carer she just didn't find a suitable match and remained a spinster like her sister Brinda, but she was able to have a house to herself close to the family home in Kurseong. Her good looks attracted the attention of a few young men who vied with each other for her hand but she continued to ward off any suggestion of marriage. So was it a fear of dominant men or a reluctance to give up her freedoms that in the end did not make things work out? Or was she really all that reserved?

Some Wikileaks showed she had at least a one-off fling with an old school friend who had spent a night with her. All that the neighbors heard was pretty loud laughter late into the night, and signs that someone had finally entered Deena's secret world. It must been more than just some relaxed moments because the maid who worked for her found that a man had stayed over for the first time. She also noticed that there were beer bottles and glasses lying around. It was also the first time that the maid had to knock to get Deena to open the door to let her in. It was also the only time she had seen Deena still in her nighties in the morning.

In fact it was noticeable that Deena tried to hide her blushes whenever the family ganged in to tease her about her lost lover, Dharmen, the guy who had visited her that night. But in the end no prospective bachelor could carry Deena off her feet.

Lynda, who seemed to be the only one somewhat fortunate, found a partner, but the relationship didn't last long because her husband was accidentally killed in a road accident on the Pankhabari® Road. Some time before he passed away she had pressed her husband to adopt two orphan children. They wanted a boy and a girl. So they approached the nuns of a convent-school® in Kalimpong.

"Sister, we are interested in adopting two children, a boy and a girl," was Lynda's request.

"We can try and help you, but we will have to find out more about how suitable you are as parents," said Sister Superior.

"Yes, of course, Sister," she replied.

After the required enquiries and procedures, Lynda and her husband were able to get to adopt Darshu and Sita from the convent. Darshu turned out to be a problem, just two years after Lynda and her husband had taken him in at the age of 8. He picked up unwelcome habits like drug-taking and continued for many years to harass the family. Sita, two years younger to Darshu, on the other hand, found a partner eventually and helped her mother in her clothing and hostel business.

Lynda had links with traders and business folk and had a rather flourishing clothing outlet at her hostel premises to sell to those who came by as well as to other shoppers in the area. The hostel was very much a sort of Bed & Breakfast set-up and because of the many travelers who needed one-night stops this part of the business too was doing well. Darshu also found a partner much later, but that didn't seem to steady him. He did little for his mother's business and wasn't really a support to her.

Billu Singh turned out to be the most enterprising of the three sons of Ratan and Chandni. He took after his father and got into forestry. Soon he moved away temporarily from Kurseong to Ghum, to learn the trade. He got a junior posting in Soonadah, and he and Chula set up home there. As the children came along they found it inconvenient for schooling and for child care. They struggled with providing for their first child, Laila. The small convent school nearby served for the first two years of primary school. But the couple was looking for better standards, and when the second girl, Saima, came along, some years later, child care problems added to their school issues.

So Billu and Chula decided that Billu should take up a small flat or a room perhaps, in Soonadah, while Chula would move back to Kurseong to the family home there. The school situation there was much better, with a convent and high school nearby and with much better nursing and child care facilities. However Chula was not all that comfortable with leaving Billu alone in Soonadah. She had hints from her female friends that he could go off on a fling as he was quite a hunky star with women.

Chula was aware that she had to take risks and so had asked Saara, in the Soonadah resort, to keep an eye on Billu. Little did she realize that Saara, mature as she looked, was as desirable to men as she desired comfort, both from wandering traders and from hunky men like Billu. Yes, she was no angel. Saara had in fact tried on the odd occasion to lure Billu into situations that could have made people suspicious that there was something going on between them. Menopause hadn't really blunted her sharpness in business or her willingness for the occasional fling, provided it was all discreetly done.

On one occasion Billu was back late from his trips and had dropped by at Saara's resort just for a drink. That evening there were very few drinkers, and none of them of Billu's acquaintance. As soon as this lot had gone Saara came and offered Billu one more drink, on the house. She sat opposite Billu literally gazing into his eyes. She could notice that he looked lonely and though she hadn't really dressed to kill, she had on a seductive-looking low-necked top anyway. She wasn't the one usually who made the first moves, but she and Billu knew each other reasonably well and getting closer to him was quite easy really. She often asked Billu for advice on some financial and on some personal issues and he was quite friendly to talk to. That had brought them quite close together in many ways.

Billu too had often spoken to her of his troubles at work and gradually he also threw in a little bit of how there was a measure of coldness in his relations with Chula creeping in. Saara too always felt comfortable talking to Billu about her business problems and about other issues. On this evening though, the two pairs of eyes seemed to show a particular fondness when they met. As she tenderly looked into Billu's eyes, Saara noticed a certain longing, and so she took the initiative. She soon edged nearer to Billu's side and the two were soon comfortable in each other's arms.

It had been quite some time that Saara hadn't got close to a man, but with Billu it was different. Their closeness had grown. In the stillness of the night, in the dimly-lit room the fondness the couple had for each other just led on to a much closer physical bonding. However, nothing much happened beyond some passionate hugging that night. Yet when they parted in the morning both knew that they needed a more intimate date. But there was nothing to suggest that they had shared more intimate moments any other time.

Chula and Saara meanwhile had become good friends, and Chula never wanted to dig deep. She just wanted Saara to keep some sort of surveillance on Billu, more to protect him than to report any misbehaviour. She had never doubted Saara's honesty.

"How are you?" Chula once made a quick call to Saara.

"I'm fine....and how are you getting on with the children?"

"Pretty well, but of course, it isn't easy with so much going on....Really wanted to know how Billu was doing."

"He's fine, from what I know," said Saara, though

she was hiding the fact that she and Billu had enjoyed a relaxing night only about a week earlier. Women of course know how to maintain their deep secrets especially when they're still emotionally involved. "Don't worry. I'll keep an eye on him. He's a good guy, so don't worry," she assured Chula.

But Chula hadn't calculated that a certain Sudha would be coming by, to the resort, some months after she'd moved to Kurseong.

Billu soon got an offer to take up government contracts, and gradually changed his work from forest officer, like his father, to contractor and builder. The takings were far better and with a growing family Billu thought that this was his future.

The problems began when Billu didn't return home at some weekends. Moreover, after their third child, again a girl, Bindya, Chula's recovery was slow and her bonding with Billu seemed to slip away gradually, though it was apparently not deliberate. Her daily chores took quite a toll on her while she found it exhausting to match Billu's different needs. There were times he had returned quite tired and somewhat depressed from his government contracts looking for Chula's support both moral and physical, but Chula, besides catering diligently to his general wellbeing could not meet her conjugal obligations to his satisfaction.

So, when Sudha became a regular employee in Saara's resort, things began looking up for Billu. At first he just treated Sudha as the regular waitress and helper. Soon, as she found him lonely and depressed, she deftly moved forward and began to take control. She would often stay on late to chat with Billu. Initially it was just friendly chat about anything and everything. Then she found he was taking an interest in her when he began asking her to do small favours for him like getting something from the local market, or perhaps getting a special dish cooked for him. He found her more than obliging and soon she began forseeing his needs. He just didn't know how to thank her for her constant attentions. He didn't suspect that a teenager would be interested in him, a middle-aged business man nearly twice her age.

There were occasions she delivered his requests, or perhaps even his meal, to the room he used to stay in occasionally, when he didn't feel like getting back to his rented room in the town. There were times when she would put on special make-up or perfume when she took things into his room. Needless to say Billu noticed this with a certain sense of satisfaction, and patted her gently or squeezed her hand or showed some other sign of appreciation.

Saara didn't really pick up on all this action going on between the two, though she knew that Billu was getting fond of Sudha. But Chula kept in touch with Saara to get a feedback on how her husband was doing, even though he wasn't staying permanently at the resort. Chula began to get a bit restless when Billu did not turn up one weekend. He had made a phone call to a friend of Chula's to inform her that he would be busy with work that weekend

Chula had other friends in Soonadah who would also keep her informed about Billu's movements. That particular afternoon Billu didn't go to work. When that happened invariably he would book a room in the resort. Chula was aware of that. So as soon as Chula got wind of Billu not going to work she sensed he would be at the resort. Her Wikileaks information earlier confirmed the facts about Sudha's getting close to Billu and about Billu's behavior patterns in Soonadah. Chula didn't lose any time. Kurseong is only about 30 minutes away by road from Soonadah. So, she took off in a flash and was in time to discover the love-struck couple canoodling on the terrace.

Chapter 4
The Railway Connection

There were certainly some caring trends in the family. Not only did Brinda become a nurse, her niece, Laila, Billu's daughter, also went into nursing later. Much earlier, Ratan's sister, Amla, too had worked in a railway hospital as a nurse. Amla was a quiet but diligent worker, always conscious of her work and responsibility, a very committed nurse. She had spent most of her working years on the Assam-Bengal Railways that operated largely in the Assam area, quite far away from and to the north east of their ancestral home in Kurseong.

Assam is a state bordering on Bengal, to the north east of India. It is quite a defense-sensitive area for India as it borders on China and Nepal to the north, Burma (Myanmar) to the east and Bangladesh sort of squeezed in between Bengal on its west and Assam on its east. The British as a colonial power had strategically linked Assam to Bengal and to the rest of India because of the logistical movement of troops and equipment. They had also set up hospitals and recovery areas for their troops all along the route. Darjeeling and Kurseong had excellent facilities. But Guwahati®, the capital of Assam, a railway centre as well, had an equally good hospital, adequate for the needs in Assam.

One of Amla's assignments was to this railway hospital. Just a 30-hour run by train, Guwahati was not too far away for Amla from her relatives in Kurseong. As a nurse she was given the special care of a railway officer, Gerry Gomes. He had come in with a heart problem as well as with other complications which included some signs of diabetes, high BP and high cholesterol. Amla was more than skilled at her work, and her dedication not only helped Gerry pull through his ill health but it also brought him closer to Amla. Gerry, from Goa®, had most of his family, brothers and sisters, away in England or Canada. He was about the only one in India, and at 40 he was quite the bachelor available. It didn't take long before Amla accepted his proposal, and they were soon a couple.

Gerry took interest in the wider family of Amla established in Kurseong though he and Amla were not able to have children of their own. Soon Gerry Gomes found Siliguri, at the foot-hills of the Himalayas, in the Darjeeling-Kurseong region, a warmer clime than Kurseong. He decided to establish a home there but continued to visit his in-laws in Kurseong as often as he could. However

Gerry would also occasionally visit his cousins in Goa, Bangalore® and Mumbai®. On some of these visits, whenever he could arrange for them, he took along with him one or both of Billu's the two elder girls, Laila and Saima. The two girls gradually made friends with the younger children of his cousins and they were soon in contact by letter with these families. The girls took a liking to Goa, and soon got fond of the two boys, Nilesh and Dinesh, sons of one of his cousins, the DeCruzes.

Not all was well for Sudha and Billu. Sudha besides being an orphan had never had very much schooling. It would seem that she might have completed the first two years of primary school before her father passed away. But she had learnt it all the common way, the hard way, looking after her mother and caring for and grooming her younger brother. She was street-wise but, after officially marrying Billu, she had moved up a few places in the social ladder, and had become the rightful heir to all the family property and power of this reasonably well-established family of Kurseong.

Even Brinda, Deena and Lynda had to show some sense of deference to Sudha though she was fit to be their daughter. Though they were aware that she had had no formal education they were in a way compelled to take the lead from her when it came to family matters. Billu in fact let her take many of the clan's decisions, and did his best to promote her, as he was away for most of the time at his work in the Ghum area or elsewhere. Sudha had common sense enough to respect all the elders in the family, including Biru, Billu's eldest brother and Balti his wife, both powerful players in family matters.

Gradually as Sudha's ties with the family grew she appeared to settle in better, and soon she and Billu had a child. This one too was a girl, Ponda: her own child, the one who would give a kind of legitimacy to her place in the clan. Ponda would now be the objective of her attentions, of her plans, of her future. In fact, her entire focus, to some extent even more than on Billu, was on her beloved Ponda. Sudha was determined that Ponda would have the best, no matter what it cost. There was nothing too expensive or outlandish for her beloved: the fruit of her union with Billu.

Billu, too busy in his projects and completely trusting in Sudha, did not realize that he was now more under petticoat control than he had ever been before even under Chula. He was now nearly totally henpecked, giving in even to some of the crazy wishes of Sudha. Though Billu continued to take advice from Brinda, Deena and Lynda he really only listened to Sudha. In fact, these three senior women had little say in all that developed over the next few years either in family issues or in the bringing up of Ponda.

The child was one of the secret achievements of Sudha in her botched secret master plan: a blood bond to take over the great Singh family. Ponda now became a reason for Sudha to get properly inserted into the family traditions. She ensured that all the rights and privileges possible of the Singh clan were given or bequeathed to Ponda, including all property, possessions and inheritance, and she kept ensuring that all financial policies too were properly registered in Ponda's name.

The ones short-changed were Billu's three children from Chula: Laila, Saima and Bindya. For all practical purposes they became second-class citizens in the Singh household, even though rightfully they were the three elder children of Billu. The first one to realize this was Laila who had gone off to do her nursing studies. She didn't seem too keen on returning home to Kurseong even to see her sisters and her dad because she had heard of developments back home where Sudha was really controlling all the moves. After completing her nursing she was able to get a fairly lucrative and prestigious job in the Tata Hospital in Jamshedpur®. She stayed on there for a few years, only visiting home for a few weeks every year.

Her sister, Saima, who hadn't done as much training, went through a series of trials for jobs. She first sought her fortunes closer to home, in secretarial work in Kurseong, and then took up short assignments in teaching in Kalimpong, in Soonadah and finally in a small primary school, run by her friend of hers, in Darjeeling. However because she was not really trained as a teacher she didn't feel comfortable in teaching jobs.

Meanwhile, during her Kalimpong teaching days, she had enrolled for an Arts degree through distance learning and private study. During her Darjeeling primary school teaching she was able to complete the degree. Just then one of the applications she sent out was accepted by a company. She was shortlisted, and was soon a Call Center worker in Mumbai, quite a long way away from home. That's where luck brought in some possibility of a permanent change for her, even though she felt comfortable in the job.

Call Center work became quite a lucrative proposition in India in the nineties. Multi-national companies in the USA, the UK and other European countries found it cost effective to operate from India. Satellite communication systems made that possible. Moreover India because of its colonial past had English well inserted into the education system and so many students with university education could speak and use English intelligibly enough for 'westerners' (mainly UK and USA speakers) to understand. So applicants from India stood a better chance of employment in Call Centers than those from many other countries around the world. In addition the pay packet was good for the average Indian worker. An average Call Centre worker in India got around Rs.15,000 [app.£190 or $250] a month, which was nearly twice or 2 ½ times the average salary of a low-paid blue-collar worker or medium-salaried technician.

On one of the trips of Gerry Gomes to Goa, when he had taken along the two girls, Laila and Saima, he had stayed with his cousin in the Margao area, close to the railway station. On that occasion, Saima couldn't stay on for more than a fortnight, but Laila just had to hang on while Gerry completed all his chores for property and other business. During one of those days Gerry had asked Dinesh, his cousin's younger son, to show Laila a bit of Goa. Dinesh was more than thrilled, and took her along the narrow Goa village roads showing off his pretty pillion rider to the people in the villages he drove through. It was almost as if Gerry had played Cupid, and even though the pair hadn't really spent much time together just seeing a few sights, Dinesh felt she was a precious catch worth pursuing and waiting for. Love eventually did blossom, and some years later, the two were man and wife.

It took longer for Nilesh, the elder boy, to make up his mind. He hadn't really had a very successful campaign finding a partner, but at Dinesh's wedding he had kept a close eye on Saima. Later, after a bit of thought, and after a few trips to Mumbai, where Saima worked, he confirmed his choice. Two years after Dinesh, Nilesh and Saima tied the knot.

For Bindya, the youngest of the three daughters of Billu and Chula, there was a bit more than a roller-coaster ride. She was young and stunningly beautiful, and it wasn't a surprise when she had fallen in love passionately with Jatin, a dashing hunk, a frequent visitor to their house in Kurseong. Even before proper arrangements could be made, the two had become more than a couple in many ways. Her parents had to consent to their marriage, as she was pregnant, and was expecting twins. However, she lost them unfortunately, and the second attempt at pregnancy also failed. There was even more unpleasant news in store when her in-laws forced her to get divorced. The only silver lining to her story was that she was encouraged to take on the nursing studies arranged for her by Billu and Sudha. Here too it wasn't long before Bindya linked up with another partner, one of the students at this nursing college in Siliguri.

There is more to her story than meets the eye, as this Singh saga unfolds. Even though she and her two other sisters could be in line for any dynastic hand-me-downs in power and privileges they did not really stand a chance in the family hierarchy against the favoured pet-child of Billu and Sudha, Ponda. Ponda was being groomed very much like a film-star, perhaps modeled on popular Bollywood stars like Aiswarya Rai®, Priyanka Chopra® or Katrina Kaif®. But Ponda also fought her own corner in subtle ways, perhaps wilier than *Boadicea*® (who resisted the Roman rule in Britain) or perhaps more focused than the Rani of Jhansi® (who stood up to the British in India). She seemed to know instinctively how to get whatever she wanted. Her upbringing in a more modern high school, and her linking up with wealthier teenagers gave her outlandish tastes and expectations. Ponda showed a peculiar interest in rare fashions and expensive gadgets, and was soon the show girl of town.

Chapter 5

Himalayan Hurdles

Life was not all rosy in the Singh family, or in their relations with others, including the DeCruzes in Goa, on India's west coast. In fact it took some time for Billu to agree to Laila getting hitched to Dinesh. Laila had to an extent replaced Chula in the affections of Billu, as he periodically needed support and advice. He was a doting father who wanted her involved for a few years more before she flew off the nest, even though it was only guidance by telephone very often. She showed wisdom above her years and he trusted her counsel immensely, in some ways more than he valued Sudha's.

To add to it the proposed alliance with Dinesh, a Goan®, was not in his view a very attractive offer. Gerry Gomes, who had married his aunt Amla was also a Goan, and had not really given an exemplary account of his life to them. Though he had used his savings to support and sustain some failing flagships of the Singhs, he had also shown some unpleasant sides of himself, e.g. the whisky habit or, externally at least, a sort of freer style of living that the Singhs did not approve of, even though in reality the Singhs were not exactly lined up for sainthood. The fact is that Billu took quite some time to agree to Dinesh's request to marry Laila.

"Dinesh is a good guy, Dad," Laila pleaded.

"I know that, but see what happened to Amla. Some of these Goans have the drinking habit."

"But, Dinesh is different. He doesn't drink," Laila insisted.

Gerry and Amla who had no children decided to settle down in Siliguri in the plains in their own place, not far from Kurseong in the hills, where the Singh base was. Gerry's brothers and sisters had all moved out of the Assam area where they had worked. His sister had brought up a rather large family, of five children, in south Kolkata®, in Bengal, while his other sister had moved abroad to Canada where she too had her family of three children. Somehow Gerry got left behind probably more because he decided to stay on with Amla's extended family than because he didn't want to migrate, or to move to Goa perhaps. However Gerry continued to keep up his links with his cousins in India.

The elder girl, Laila, and Dinesh, the younger DeCruz boy, got married in Goa, but the grander celebrations took place in Kurseong. The two had reasonably good jobs in Dubai® and enjoyed a fairly successful life out there but had also invested in a small flat in Bangalore®, in southern India, because they hoped they might settle there when they retired. Two years later their first baby, Bob, had to be taken to Kurseong for the traditional 'first meal' or 'Bhaat Khawai'® celebration, which apparently is a landmark function in the Singhs as well as in other families in the hills, when a child gets welcomed by the wider clan. The function is really about the 'feeding (khawai) of the first morsel (bhaat-rice) to the baby' to mark the end of the period of breast feeding.

The celebration, in the Himalayan region, assumes great significance culturally and takes on other rituals. Besides the 'feeding' the other rituals include fussing over the baby, getting the baby's head shaven, passing the baby around to all the grandees for their blessings, spreading a lavish table for friends and community around, and promoting the family's name, fame and influence through the displays of buntings and gifts and the presence of important guests. All this is the equivalent of a near-royal celebration in this relatively remote Darjeeling-Kurseong hill region.

Darjeeling itself, about 80 km from Siliguri in the plains was set up as a resort area by the British when they were in India. They used it as the centre for medical attention for their soldiers wounded in their many skirmishes with Rajas® and kingdoms in the rest of India. The little narrow-gauge railway from Darjeeling to Siliguri connected with the meter-gauge railway, that passed Siliguri junction, both from Bengal and from Assam, and brought these soldiers or other travelers and tourists to Kurseong and Darjeeling.

About 30 km before reaching Darjeeling, at about 2000 metres, from Siliguri in the plains, is Kurseong, at about 1500 meters, also a resort area. Both towns also had several educational institutions patterned on the British Public School® system of the UK. Darjeeling had St Paul's run by the Anglicans®, St Joseph's conducted by the Jesuits®, Loreto Convent run by the Loreto® nuns and Mount Hermon's, which later also became a TTC® college, conducted by the Methodists®.

Kurseong had Goethals school for boys run by the Christian Brothers® and St Helen's Convent for girls set up by Daughters of the Cross® (a French Order of nuns), and two government sponsored schools: Dowhill Girls' School and Victoria School for boys. Later on St Alphonsus's technical school was also set up there by the Jesuits. At one time the Jesuits also had their Theologate®, the final four years of training for Catholic priests, on St Mary's Hill in Kurseong.

Laila and Saima had both done their High School at St Helen's Convent and Laila especially shone in all her work. In fact she attracted the attention of the nuns who thought she might be a good candidate for the Order. One day Sister Carol, the Superior asked her,

"Laila, would you like to work for other children?"

"What do you mean?" asked Laila, who didn't have a clue as to what Sister Carol wanted to know.

"You know what I mean. I think you're a good girl and a good leader too. We think you could become a good Sister one day, teaching other girls, the way we do."

It did come as a bit of a surprise to Laila, but she took it in her stride and told Sister Carol, "I'll think about it Sister."

"Yes, you should. You'd be very good. The children would love you, and you would feel happy to be able to do some good to others."

Laila kept it to herself for a while, but then later decided to talk to her father about Sister's comment.

"Give it some time. You're too young now. I think you'll be a good mother to your own children," said her father. "You can decide about it all when you've done all your studies. We'll talk about it later, maybe in a few months' time."

When Nilesh married Saima the Bhaat Khawai celebrations seem to have got more complicated as part of the wedding had to be celebrated in

Kurseong and part of it in Goa. Perhaps that is what made their Bhaat Khawai get much more elaborate in Kurseong, in early 2000. At Bagdogra, the airport closest to Kurseong, they were picked up by Billu and his youngest daughter Bindya. The drive up to Kurseong, from the beautiful tea-garden plantations around the airport, is about 40 km via the shorter route called the Pankhabari Road. The main road up, from Siliguri to Kurseong, the Hill-Cart® Road, would be at least 20 km longer. The Pankhabari Road however is so badly in need of repair that the hairpin bends can only be negotiated by drivers who have mastered the art of maneuvering those untarred and slippery roads. Before getting to Kurseong, they decided to take the opportunity to visit the new Mall in the City Centre of Siliguri, which is the second largest town in Bengal.

Bengal, one of the larger states of India, for many years under a non-effective government, had experienced a recession-like phase. The Darjeeling area, which is in north Bengal, felt the brunt of this lack of development as well as of the political wrangling of some of the new parties springing up. All this left the people confused and the infrastructure in tatters. Kurseong too was no exception and, in addition to the roads being in a state of severe disrepair and power-cuts disrupting daily living, life had become unmanageable for the average person, with lack of provisions and facilities. Even the prestigious schools in both Kurseong and Darjeeling, which also had overseas students, were now facing withdrawals and operational problems.

Siliguri itself, which is at the bottle-neck of north and south Bengal, is also the link route for several sovereign states and countries. Located really not very far away from Siliguri are independent countries: Nepal to the northwest, Bhutan to the northeast, China to the far north and Bangladesh to the south. Siliguri is also close to the Indian states of: Sikkim to the north, Bihar to the west, and Meghalaya® and Assam to the east.

People in the hill region though far off from the city lifestyle of Siliguri yet keep longing for whatever they see on TV or on the internet. Young people especially just don't bother whether their parents can afford it or not and just want the newest electronic gadget or the latest fashion wear. Ponda was always the first to check for what was available in town, i.e. Siliguri. Laila, Saima and Bindya too always had quite a few silly demands, and poor Dad, Billu, was left to figure out how to pay off these huge bills.

Though they reached Kurseong quite late, at around 8 pm when it was dark, after a bumpy drive over poor roads, via the Pankhabari route, the Bhaat Khawai couple looked eager for the celebrations. The reception, after the initial freshening up, was quite colorful and lively, with the women folk bustling around to take control, getting the children to be orderly and ensuring that the men folk had been given due attention. As part of the welcome they were garlanded with the symbolic 'kadha' scarf, and were then offered the traditional milk drink.

The small silk scarves have prayers or inscriptions on them, signifying religious or pious sayings in Christianity or in Buddhism. While the women were all fussing over the baby, the central figure of all the celebrations, refreshments were served up. This helped to keep the men folk interested and involved.

The men in the region, generally not a very knowledgeable lot, are mostly retired men from the British Gurkha® regiments, blue-collared workers doing Government jobs or just ordinary professional men not really interested in more than their jobs and in community gossip. The local brew, easily available in the local pubs, is the favorite 'pint' that they all quaff through while sitting around a fire or an electric heater while chatting away the hours!

On the next day, Nilesh tried to sort out an internet connection, using a dongle, besides looking around for some other helpful gadgets in this somewhat cut-off region to be able to stay in touch, in communication terms, with family and friends. Deena, the elder sister to Billu, who's a spinster and lives in her own house, in the bazaar area, near the family home where the couple was staying, came by to spend time with them. The other sister, the eldest, Brinda, also a spinster, who had come up from Siliguri where she has her home, was around as well to share all the family gossip. Brinda is in a way quite a respected figure as she helped many members of the family financially in difficult times. Both ladies brought gifts for the new baby, mainly toys, and stayed for most of the day. Billu's main house, not far from from Deena's house, was generally the main venue for all the family gatherings.

On the next day, the day of the Bhaat Khawai, at around 10.30 am the function officially began, with the couple seated in the reception hall, the sitting room, waiting for guests. The first to congratulate the baby was the young pair of Darshu and Sita. They came with the gift of a baby girl doll, an expensive gift, which could spin while its pre-recorded tape played some music. The toy's skirt was like an umbrella that opened up with a click, and the doll stood up on a stand which needed winding in order to operate. Everyone was quite amazed at the toy though the parents of the child couldn't really see the significance of a doll for a male child.

At the Bhaat Khawai ceremony, there was another interesting ritual that some of the younger folk especially thought had little connection with the first morsel eaten. The local barber arrived, and poor baby Lee had to have his head totally shaven. That was followed by a bath and a massage, and naturally the final dressing up before the 'feeding' bit.

The Singhs were an enigmatic family even before Sudha came on the scene. It was apparent that Biru, the eldest in the clan, and Balti his wife, were not really amassing either a fortune or any credibility. Balti had a way with people, and used her smile, her charm and her poise to keep everyone believing that she was royalty! The second boy, Shidu, had intuition enough to sense that the Singhs were heading for a financial downturn and so headed for Canada.

Billu, who thought he would be the savior of the clan, and a kind of socio-religious symbol of Biru's church projections, ran into troubled waters with his amorous adventures. His lack of commitment to Chula and the kids, his inexperience with financial arrangements and his naive approach to people and society seemed to have left a vacuum in the sorting out of issues in the Singh clan.

Sudha soon noticed that Billu often seemed lost when he had to make decisions. Billu too, almost without his realizing it, was gradually handing over all chores, decisions, money and power to Sudha. He was so emotionally involved with her that he couldn't see her to be otherwise than his guardian support and his wall of strength, one who could do no wrong in his eyes, even though she had no educational background. Whatever she suggested or recommended to him was top priority for him, sometimes even at the cost of his official work.

"Billu, dear," she asked him one day. "We need to get both our signatures down on our main account in the State Bank. Can we do it today?"

"Yes, of course," Billu agreed. And it was done. That settled her financial position.
"And how about the house insurance transfer?" she asked another day.

"We can do that next week. Is that ok?" said Billu.

"Yes, we can do it next Monday," Sudha agreed, having had her way, making sure that the properties were registered in her name as well.

The three Singh women didn't do much better than the men. Brinda was perhaps the only one who made some headway when she regularly sent back money to cash-starved Biru and to floundering Billu, not to speak of support for her sisters Deena and Lynda. Her long nursing career in Oman was about the only redeeming feature rescuing the family from sliding towards financial collapse. Deena in some sort of altruistic way cared for the family, for Lynda, and for her brothers Biru and Billu.

Both Brinda and Deena also missed out on getting married and in some ways failed the cycle of Nepali traditions. Not unlike other cultures family life and having children are essential pegs in a clan's definitive establishment and development. Brinda wanted to have children but her involvement in her work abroad and her desire to help her own relatives made her put it off for too long. Deena got too involved with looking after her parents, and it got late for her as a woman to find a match in her part of the world. Lynda's marriage unfortunately failed because her husband passed away, and her efforts to rescue it with two adoptions did very little to stem the tide of misfortunes dogging this family.

Chapter 6

Himalayan Ways

The people in the hill region which includes Darjeeling, Kurseong, Kalimpong, Mirik and all the surrounding areas between Sikkim and Nepal, and the plains of Bengal, would appear to have developed their own ways of dealing with friends and family, with opponents and enemies, with situations and occasions, and with opportunities and offers. Travelling and communicating on the hills has always posed a challenge because of the difficult mountain terrain, the inaccessible roads and paths and the uncertainties of wild life in the area. There are also hazards of landslides, of treacherous storms or worse still of armed gangs. Yet traditions and cultural habits, e.g. the Bhaat Khawai, seem to be passed on and continued in spite of communication hassles.

Survival strategies however on these mountains still take on vital importance. Telephone communication and the wireless, or radio, were and probably still are the quickest ways to reach people. But there is also a certain patience that seems to be built into the psyche of these people. Almost nothing seems to ruffle them, and in good times and bad they support each other almost to the hilt, even if no news comes through or if nothing seems to happen. All the same there is a certain sluggishness or perhaps cautiousness that underpins this pattern of life that cannot be identified to a certainty that would seem to hinder progress and development.

People get their water from the hills, their produce from the rice beds on the hill-sides, their tea from the slopes on the hills, their prayer-filled hopes from the prayer-flags flying from poles on the hill sides (a Buddhist belief). They probably believe that 'help will come from on high', as David® sang in the Bible®. That, in more rational times, meant that mixed messages could be floating around in the mist that so abundantly fills these hills. The Vestal Virgins® knew how to tell Alexander when to go to war and when to use more subtle tactics. In today's world, on the hills, where education is just about getting to hidden corners of this semi-intractable region, wise 'gurus' continue to wander around proclaiming mantras and tantric messages, influencing naive men and women who are constantly looking for answers. Is their traditional patience wearing thin? Or is there a changing pattern emerging?

It is perhaps an area that has religion and culture so inextricably linked that it is difficult to assess if gurus or tradition hold the day. In some ways it becomes easier to follow tradition, because at the end of it there will be a celebration where no one or perhaps nothing is questioned. This is perhaps not so different in other places in the world, as in parts of Africa, Asia or Latin America, or even Europe perhaps, where community matters and everything else is secondary or not worth bothering about.

However, with Billu's parents migrating from the Bihar region to the hill region of Darjeeling, and then later with Billu's linking up with a totally different culture, by marrying Sudha, of Sikkimese stock, there was certainly a moving of the plates. It is true that Billu's parents settled into the hill region over more than 40 years before Billu got entangled with Sudha, but somehow people never really grow off their roots, or perhaps are predictable to a point quite similar to the way the undulating paths on mountains always seem to stay that way. So also weeds grow alongside plants, and sometimes there is no way of telling one from the other, as Billu would certainly have found out from his forestry work in his younger days.

So, at the Bhaat Khawai festivities, there was nothing to suggest it was either a Bihari ritual, a mountain-region style or a Nepali practice that had made up the choice of events. It would seem that it was a celebration that had become part and parcel of the traditions that had been communicated across families and handed down. Some of these traditions are never questioned or analyzed and they soon become folk culture. The younger folk, even in this sort of remote region who live in their own worlds, influenced by gadgets or underground currents, like drugs, have additional pressures put on them. With both parents working or with hardly anyone at home to guide their options as they grow up, it would seem that many of them just get on to whatever comes by, e.g. a chance or a deal.

So it was when Darshu and Sita had come along with their doll gift. Along with the doll the pair had brought in 3 open envelopes, two of which had letters: one for the parents of the baby boy, one for the baby boy and a third envelope which had cash in it. Soon after they had come by there was a phone call to the couple from Deena to check if the cash envelope had reached. When they did check the envelope, they were quite shocked to learn that there should have been Rs.1000 in it instead of the Rs.500 they found inside. It was not convenient at the time to find out why Darshu and Sita had acted so irresponsibly.

The couple found out later Darshu was into drugs and, in all probability the toy that was given to them was bought for around Rs.200 or a little more, with the rest of the money pocketed by the young pair. Without labeling people, this sort of mismanagement of money is a constant worry when dealing with people in the region, especially with the younger adults who constantly seem to be looking for opportunities to short-change people they deal with.

Darshu was also known to have been pilfering money from the cash box of his mother's business. He had to feed his drug habit, grass, which was easily available in the Kurseong area at the time. It is strange that he did not become an alcoholic with alcohol too easily available in a few licensed shops, including the Bed & Breakfast joint of his mother. What he needed really was money to get access to these drugs. So if he found opportunities he had no scruples. What was the more serious problem was that he got violent after the drugs, and there were times when he had to be quarantined off in a locked room, and had to be kept there until the effect of the drugs had worn off. In those violent moods, because of the drugs he had taken, no one could approach him or control him.

In a similar way, some marriage arrangements and affairs do not figure prominently in open discussion in this region. It just sort of occurs. It happens for example when a man steps forward to rescue a woman from painful situations. The case we know of is Darshu's wife, who was already a married woman, a former sales girl, when he married her. She had been married to a guy who had ill-treated her. She lived bang opposite to his adopted mother's house. Hearing her cries as she was being beaten and seeing the injuries she suffered he fell for her. She was a pretty woman too, kind and considerate, who to the people around, especially to Darshu, deserved to be rescued.

For Darshu's wife it was welcome relief, and she soon got attached to him because he sought to rescue her from harm and because his mother had money to support her and perhaps give her a job as well. Darshu decided that in order to rescue her he had to marry her. These easy adjustments to relationships seem to be the acceptable practice in this region. Sita, his sister, was a little steadier as a person, and her partner would appear to have supported Lynda more than Darshu did.

A further interesting practice, on these hills, not very dissimilar, is the one where when a boy can elope with a girl without too many hassles. All he has to do is stay away for three days or more, to prove that he could support her, and then he could earn the right to marry her and get back into favour with the wider family. Usually a senior member of the boy's family then has to track down the eloping couple, visit them, and work out a peace-strategy with them and the two families. He then gets both parties to accept the marriage, and the boy and his girl are accepted back into the two families and into society.

This is exactly what happened to Prakar, Biru's third son, who had to elope with the girl of his choice so that he could marry her. He had taken to drugs, and was nearly a lost cause. Smita, a pretty girl, a social worker and teacher, took pity on Prakar and gradually brought him to his senses. She was able to get him out of his drug addiction but in the process she fell in love with him. However, she was not what the Singhs believed was their type of girl because, pretty and stunning as she was, she was not a Christian. Prakar kept trying to convince them that all would be well finally, but failed, and so had to take the 'hill option'—elope.

Closer to the family, Bindya too followed a similar route. Bindya had eloped after doing her Year 12 final exam at school. She ran away for 3 days with the boy she was infatuated with, Jatin. They spent the 'accepted' 3-day-away method, in a hotel. This was quite a shock for Billu, as he had high hopes for her. She was really his beloved daughter, his little beauty. He couldn't understand what had gone wrong. But at this point in time he had to 'rescue' her by bringing her back and then taking her to Jatin's family. They were then formally married. Things didn't work out all that well though, as she was forced to do all the menial work in the boy's house in Mirik, from cleaning and sweeping to washing clothes and water-filling, which proved to be extremely strenuous for her.

Bindya's case indeed is one of those Himalayan tales too pitiful to retell. The strain of the work took its toll on her, and eventually it made her lose her twins. In spite of all the inhospitable attitude of Jatin's family, a second pregnancy followed, but that proved disastrous as well, as she lost that baby too. The boy's family who literally continued to enslave her was now keen to get rid of her. To work that out they needed a willing agent. Bindya's story took another intriguing turn. Did nature step in or did someone intervene? There's more to this.

Meanwhile, there's more to the Bhaat Khawai function as well. The hair-cutting ritual proved quite a problem for Bob, the son of Dinesh and Laila, who screamed till his lungs had nearly come off, when he heard the sound of the clippers. Bob needed more than two stalwarts to hold him down and something close to a muzzle to silence this innocent little 'bundle of joy'! No such problems for Lee, who didn't bat an eyelid. He must have mused to himself, in his own child-intuitive way, "Don't care what they do to my hair. They mustn't touch my Mama's."

One other noticeable feature of many families in the hilly region is that quite a few of the husbands, the men folk, are out of the region for employment in other states of India or abroad. They send regular remittances to their families, and visit about once a year. These home-returns are usually marked by the arrival of a child in about 9 months after their visits. The women don't seem to mind this. It gives them time to settle into the traditions of the clan as well as to become part of the chain of gossip so that the conversations and the traditions in these hills keep going!

However, this absence of the male figure for long periods leaves the women folk at home missing the father influence on their children and the men's emotional support as well. This also leaves them exposed to evil-intentioned bachelors prowling around, and quite often breaking up homes. It is not uncommon to discover new liaisons when the working bachelors return home, or perhaps women, their wives, made pregnant during the husbands' absence from home. With the lack of infrastructure and employment development in the region this situation seems to have deteriorated. NGOs[®] and the Government could perhaps be persuaded to offer schemes where employment is provided locally for the men folk so that families could stay together.

Another interesting phenomenon is that quite a few people seem to have come through the regular rungs of education and qualification, but there is a certain amount of lack of purpose or dedication seen in the youth population especially. They're keener on attending parties and fun events than studying for their examinations and qualifications. At one point, on the eve of her very crucial Physics exam Ponda was busy decking herself up for a teenage party. When she was asked,

"Why aren't you studying for your Physics exam for tomorrow?"

"I don't need to bother," she replied. "My master [teacher] will take care of that."

It is difficult to assume anything from that reply, but how do they pass their exams? That's a million dollar question, or is there a million dollars involved somewhere? It's perhaps best not to speak of what possibilities there could be. Later, when the results were announced, Ponda had passed her exams though she didn't quite know the difference between her Physics and her Chemistry papers. But, did it matter? She had qualified, at least for that exam. One would assume that she had similar exam gambles on the way, as and when she required them. But is that the way things are done in the hills, or are these just some of those irregular incidents?

What is commendable is that education authorities at the highest level, across India, are planning measures to ensure that public exams are properly supervised, and that cheating in any form is severely punished. One of the states in India, as reported by the Times of India®, in April 2012, has taken definitive steps to check some of these malpractices. Some of the pranks that students use, to quote the paper, are: attaching currency notes to answer sheets, or writing prayers to invoke deities, copying by passing notes around, or carrying answers from guide books into the examination hall.

Some students have gone further by threatening examiners or using equipment like wireless devices to get answers into the examination place. These practices in the hill region seem to have been rampant as well, with the authority of teachers compromised as examination supervisors or as markers. The government, as quoted in the Times, has now decreed severe penalties for these students including barring them from future exams for a few years, and also slapping heavy fines on them. It is not clear if these sanctions have reached legislation in the Himalayan region, because if they did, our heroine, Ponda would indeed have to ponder her next step!

Chapter 7
Measuring Quantities

Sudha, who, it can be safe to assume, was near illiterate was however numerate to a certain level. Her sense of cash value and of total worth of goods or individuals seems to have been instinctive. She may have picked this up from her dhobi father, when she was a little girl. Time and experience honed these skills, and soon she was applying these quantitative values when dealing with people. She had, without any assistance almost, summed up the worth of the three Singh sisters, Brinda, Deena and Lynda. She knew she that she could manipulate them the way she wanted because her confidence was sky-high. She had really 'graduated' from the 'street-wise' academy, and had become proficient in ways that were shrewd and practical. She also had inputs from her rather secretive contacts on how to measure her dealings, but above all she seemed to know how to handle people who were gullible.

Sudha, not yet in her thirties knew that these ageing ladies, in their sixties and seventies, would soon be gone by the time she would see the success of her plans and strategies unfolding. She also knew that by that time her beloved Ponda, reasonably 'educated' by then, would be in a position to take over the clan as leader and dominant force. She felt confident that the supposedly educated Ponda, acting as her mentor and administrator and as her deputy of course, would one day proclaim to the villages around that the Singhs were the new royalty in residence, where Sudha was Queen, and naturally Ponda was Princess Royale!

Perhaps it might be opportune to note here one of those beliefs of people in the hills, and perhaps also of people in other parts of India, that getting a qualification is all that matters. A BA or an MA, or perhaps an M.Com or an MBA is the acceptable sign that a person is 'educated'. Education as a broader idea where upbringing, coping with society and daily living in addition to achieving qualifications does not seem to be the idea generally held in these parts. There are scores of organizations offering qualifications, and some of them even promise miracles, with just a bit of money thrown upfront as well. It's a scam of course, but young people especially find this an easy way to enjoy life and yet get qualified.

These so-called education providers offer qualifications at a price. People fall for it because they want so appear 'educated'. In these parts especially it seems to be the sure way to climb the 'education' ladder socially by acquiring qualifications. The easy availability of drugs and alcohol adds to this profligate lifestyle for quite a few youngsters. Perhaps the larger group of young people does believe in sincerity, honesty and hard work to achieve goals, but they too are constantly exposed to the temptations of this easy-going lifestyle. So, did Ponda really get educated? Or was she just dragged on by the tide? Or would it all be revealed when she would one day become Princess?

So also, would Sudha be Queen one day? So, who would be King? Without sounding fatalistic like The Hunger Games® or perhaps in fantasy land as in the Twilight® movies it is difficult to really fathom the depths of Sudha's personal or perhaps ulterior motives. Was she genuine when she trapped Billu or perhaps Gonkul earlier? It is almost impossible to get backup information about her past. She left her settings when she was just a little girl, and those who exploited her as she grew up quite enslaved her as she kept climbing her way up the social ladder. The fact seems to be that her experiences did not teach her salutary lessons. She didn't do much to groom Ponda either. For certain she did less to bring up Ponda than she had done to groom her younger brother back in Sikkim. Perhaps all the scheming she had to cope with left her little time to bring up her prized daughter. Was there a reckoning to come?

All that Sudha perhaps was schooled into was a subtle method of undermining people and attaining her objectives. It seemed to stem from an imperceptible vindictiveness that she had learned to mask with her wry smiles and her enticing ways. She could almost use Gonkul again and again, as she had a hold on him. She quickly moved to Billu who was in emotional distress, and who could well have been her father. Her programs of action though not very well planned, were targeted, drastic and destructive. She did not seem to have a definitive plan of action but she was just determined to forge ahead oblivious of the outcomes. She probably never ever felt any sense of conscience, and used subtle and seductive ways to hide her bitterness and her ruthlessness. She managed to hold herself together with a certain untutored poise that came across in a calm yet false smile that hid the deep frustrations and the constant scheming.

There is evidence to show that she was already tiring of Billu and his rather sloweddown performance level. This was probably more uncomfortable to her than it was bothering her. Her stand-by plan was even more questionable. All this came to light at the Bhaat Khawai celebrations. There were two parties held: one in the morning and one in the late evening. The morning crowd was made up of those who attended Biru's church or Billu's business gatherings. It was a fairly respectable crowd who could use spoons and forks and the occasional serviette, and could smile at other guests and try some shots at conversation.

In fact most of them, the so-called 'intelligentsia'

of the region, would not be able to sustain an intelligent conversation beyond a few minutes, even on most ordinary topics like the weather, the latest trends in fashion or the most recent price hikes of consumables. These individuals invested in looking presentable and important and then of course drinking branded liquor and eating buffet meals prepared by reputed catering outlets. It was more about show than substance.

On the other hand, at the second party, the crowd who turned up late into the evening was like a rabble, or refugees who hadn't seen food or decency for decades, and who in church terms were like the Israelites® in the desert, giving Moses® a hard time. However, they were, according to Sudha, regular church goers. She preferred to call them her 'Society'.

This crowd of more than about 100 people was like ravenous wolves tearing at the sumptuous and daintily prepared meal laid out for them. That brilliantly-presented tantalizing food was a scene they had never been trained to handle. They loaded their plates with everything on offer, and for fear of missing out on dishes, had heaped it all up on the same plate: rice, vegetables, meat, fish all stacked up with the dessert and the ice cream topping it all! It all looked a lot like the snow at the top of volcanic Mount Kilimanjaro® in Tanzania®.

What later became evident was that Sudha used this group of 'plebeians'® (very much like the crowd that stood in the front rows at Shakespeare's® play performances in his day), to act as her confidants and her bodyguards when she needed them. They looked more like a band of bodybuilders ready for action rather than a group of well-wishers at a party. As could be expected, within minutes of the first-come-first-served group literally 'attacking' the dishes prepared, there was hardly anything left for the second round of hungry-looking Sudha-invitees.

The crudeness with which this entire group handled and ate the food spoke of their upbringing and of the settings they came from. There is nothing demeaning to belong to a poorer group of society who are not trained into sophisticated manners. It was about Sudha supposedly stooping to any lengths to use brawn power and subtle moves to sustain her objectives. Was this really the back-up that Sudha needed for her plans?

It is possible to trace the hand of Sudha in nearly every development in the family. One of the most notable ones is the way she was trying to cope with the three daughters of Chula. The two bigger girls sorted themselves out, with their marriages to the two DeCruz boys, thankfully before Sudha could have a say in their futures. The problem really was the youngest girl, Bindya. After she had eloped she nearly brought on the wrath of the entire Singh clan. All the elder women, Brinda, Deena and Lynda, and Sudha of course, were annoyed. Billu played the compassionate father, but could not hide his shock and disbelief. He did as much for her as he could, but he was not able to control the situation in the boy's, Jatin's, house.

Bindya had become a slave, at the beck and call of the mother-in-law, who kept railing against her and lambasting her with the eloping issue that her son wasn't really to blame. She then insisted that Bindya would do all the menial work at home: from washing up dishes to doing the laundry, from sweeping and cleaning to carrying water from about 100 meters away from the house. This heavy strain took its toll on Bindya whose pregnancy with the twins she was carrying had to be terminated. Once again, Jatin's mother put all the blame squarely on Bindya for this unfortunate development.

Within a year Bindya got pregnant again, and this time, for no plausible reason except that she wanted to take special care of Bindya, Sudha became a frequent visitor to the house. She didn't really have any medical background even though she had information from nurses in the family, yet she insisted on advising and taking special care of Bindya. Eventually when the facts were out it was discovered that the mother-in-law colluded with Sudha to get Bindya to abort. It would, in their sinister plot, be understandable and believable to a gullible public since Bindya had lost her baby earlier. Both of them used pressure on the doctor, against all sound medical advice, to prescribe tablets for Bindya in the fifth month of pregnancy that would hasten the abortion.

In spite of the best efforts of the Wikileaks group the doctor's prescriptions could not be found. The labels on the bottles had been cleverly removed, possibly by the mother-in-law. Sudha of course played the innocent carer, and kept insisting that the tablets were meant to give energy and strength to Bindya so that she could recover, though Bindya complained only of pain and suffering after taking the tablets. The scans in the fourth month showed a healthy child, while the scans of the sixth month showed the fetus was dead, ready for an abortion.

It was not possible to get to the bottom of this as Sudha did a few more trips to the mother-in-law to squash any leaks. But the Wikileaks group persisted in the search, and contacted a nurse, a friend of Bindya, who worked in the same clinic as the doctor. She was able to find out that the doctor had given similar prescriptions to other women who ended up being in pain. That gave away the name of the drug. It was found that these tablets were meant for pregnant women preparing to abort a fetus, and generally caused severe pain. They were definitely not meant to give any energy.

So the fairly conclusive assumption was that it must have been Sudha in collusion with the mother-in-law, who had worked it all out. Given the awkward position in which Billu was it was uncomfortable to report it to the police. Moreover Billu, unaware as he was of any plot and naïve to any suggestion of foul play, seemed to have had no options but to believe Sudha. However Brinda, with her nursing background, had strong suspicions that Sudha's story didn't add up. Her weakening health did not allow her to pursue this further.

Meanwhile Sudha, undeterred by any rumors circulating, continued her visits to this family with some frequency. Bindya reported later how the two, Sudha and the mother-in-law were together all the time that Sudha spent at the house. If, as her story to the Singh grandees went, Sudha was visiting Bindya to look after her, then she should have spent time with her. Nothing of the sort happened. It could then be reasonably assumed that Sudha was only colluding with the mother-in-law on how to get Bindya thrown out of the house. That eventually happened, and Billu once again just believed everything that Sudha told him.

Quite true to character Billu didn't know how to react. So, at Sudha's instructions, he promptly came and took Bindya away. Back at home Sudha was throwing hints at Bindya constantly, really in quite a double-faced way, that she was a burden to the house. Ponda too, with Sudha's tutoring, was making the situation even worse. Ponda kept complaining that Bindya was taking away some of her privileges, though really she wasn't getting anything less for the wasteful spending she was accustomed to.

Finally, Sudha worked out an arrangement with a college in Siliguri, and got Bindya admitted into a nursing college, with boarding arrangements as well. There too Sudha didn't leave Bindya alone. She kept visiting the college regularly supposedly –as reported to the Singh female grandees-- to support Bindya, but really it was to harass and to keep tabs on her. It was brought to Sudha's notice that some man or boy was seen with Bindya roaming through the town. Whether it was true or not it was tangible evidence for Sudha once again to start spreading all sorts of rumours about Bindya with the elders of the clan, especially Brinda, Deena and Balti.

Sudha's objective was to stop Bindya from her studies, something that strangely enough she herself had set up, because at that point in time it was costing too much. She added to these rumours that Bindya wasn't really meant for studying, a sort of repetitive melody that she kept playing to the grandees of the clan. Actually the facts were that Bindya was doing very well in her studies, and had in reality excelled in several of the recent assessments she'd done.

Sudha, who was quite accomplished at creating rumours and then spreading them systematically, often went a step further, and convinced the targeted individuals to believe that what was reported was actually happening. She was relentless in pursuing her objectives. She kept shuttling to Siliguri, to Bindya at her course, to convince her that studies were not meant for her and that she should get married again. Back with the elders she played the innocent go-between, who was trying to do her best for the clan and for Bindya.

The female grandees who had their own ageing problems just continued to believe her. She was careful to do her follow-ups, which consisted in visiting each of these senior women, and taking care of their chores at home on the odd occasion. To add to this she always told each of them the same story and made it believable. All this was enough to convince these grandees that she was the genuine product, truly compassionate and really supportive, and above all an integral part of the Singh clan traditions and decisions.

In-laws are generally introduced to the wider family gradually. Their way of life, over a period of time, has to blend into the mainstream of the family they marry into. They then adapt their individual needs and tastes into what the broader environment suggests. They are careful to appear normal and standard, and do not in any way want to stick out as sore thumbs. Within a relatively short time they take on the reputation, or otherwise, of their new family.

Yet for all their adaptation they are for most practical purposes still unknown quantities, till the wider public, and the discerning community, and especially the bastions of tradition in the family accept them as total insiders. That can take anything from six months to a year, or perhaps more. If that doesn't happen the boat moves away from its moorings. How far then had Sudha got on in this process? Was she getting closer or were there some chinks in the armor? Time would tell.

Chapter 8
Himalayan Opportunities

Billu and Sudha had dreamt up a life of buoyant adventure and success. Billu with all his experience in forestry was perhaps aware that there could be destructive and poisonous plants and trees that could endanger the lives of better species of plants and trees. His experience in business had also taught him perhaps that business partners cannot always be trusted. Yet, here was a challenge to his sense of judgement that had been clouded over by intense passion and attachment. Billu had gone through several years of living with Chula, his wife, and of bringing up his daughters, several years of rearing a family. In all those years the possibility of life without his wife or his children had never occurred to him, but the playbacks of his somewhat dodgy past were now disturbingly affecting his thinking.

He had taken his chances at the Soonadah resort, and had nearly linked up with Saara. Saara had loved his charms, and had found his virility attractive and somewhat seductive. The two had played their games but had stopped short of the final link up. Billu had a string of attachments that Saara or for that matter almost anyone else knew of.

On other occasions, he showed he had restraint, but it was always a struggle. When a group of industrialists had come to camp close to the business site, one of the women in that team had strayed out of the camp into the forest. Billu out on an exploratory job had accidentally come upon her lost in the same forest area towards dusk, and had rescued her. Billu whose reactions were pretty casual showed his chivalry as well as his charms because the safety of someone was in question. The woman, whom he took to his tent, needed a lot of reassurance and human comfort to feel secure.

Quite surprisingly within moments of her being rescued she felt safe with Billu. What surprised Billu too was that as soon as he took her into his makeshift tent she wouldn't stop weeping, all the while hugging him as well. She had apparently wandered off because she was hurt by the studied ill-treatment of her husband at home and at the camp, and just fell for Billu's kindness and gentleness, and his charms of course. She didn't know how to thank him for saving her, and for offering her such warm hospitality.

As the night wore on she felt more comfortable with him and his caring ways. Billu was cautious about taking advantage of the situation but she came on to him, almost like a woman in emotional distress, looking for understanding and support. The more she felt his manly arms protecting her the more she got drawn to him. Surprisingly, Billu was able to calm her down and to put her to rest.

The next morning her worried husband and the search party were relieved to find her, and were extremely grateful to Billu for caring for her. There weren't any telltale signs that the pair had enjoyed any erratic blissful pleasures of a 'midsummer night's dream'® in a forest tent. For the lady it had been true salvation and relief. She didn't know how to thank Billu for his nobility and kindness.

Billu had gradually developed this protective coat of arms of heroism and manliness that seemed to make him look invincible and naturally attractive to women. There was a string of women he had charmed and 'balmed'. What it was not certain to establish was how many skeletons there might have been in the cupboard. He was just hoping, while Chula was with him that she would not dig deep. With Sudha it was another story. Sudha herself was one of these women who had stolen him away from his legal first wife.

Sudha was smart but slimy as well. She followed Billu like a hawk, but she was soon sensing that Billu was beginning to fade out of her life as he was not really satisfying her. She found he was ageing in his fifties, while she had all the vigour of youth in her twenties. Billu would often come home tired after all his work and travels. Their nights of love were short and somewhat unsatisfying. She found his passion cooling off and his intensity weak. It is true they had had their first child, but Sudha, the ever-restless tigress, was constantly on the prowl.

She went for what she knew she could handle. She linked up with Gonkul once more, and timed it perfectly, just when Billu was away on duty for about 3 days. She found time and opportunity to meet up with Gonkul, this time in Kurseong, in a distant lodge, a taxi-distance away. The pretense had to be believable, so it was arranged for an afternoon. She felt she needed the release, though the entire episode did not prove to be what she was looking for. She found Gonkul too to have aged quite a bit, and to have lost interest in her. He was the more serious type and did not want to rock the boat. Instead of falling for her charms on this occasion he tried to convince her to look after her family. She found this hard to swallow, but unexpectedly in the middle of this disappointment a ray of hope lit up her path, possibly a way out of the gloom.

At the lodge she also bumped into a more energetic Bhutanese owner of this new lodge. She found him much younger, closer to her age. Simba was just 30, running his father's business, and was quite lonely outside his comfort zone of friends from Bhutan, working with people he didn't really know. Simba and Sudha just met up for a casual chat but both seemed to like each other, and soon they set up a date. Sudha couldn't believe her luck as she felt Simba was the sort of younger partner she was looking for, bright and enterprising. Sudha had just about hit 28, and was eager to continue developing her plan for her kingdom in Kurseong! Sudha found this spot, the lodge, near enough to her house too and yet far enough for any gossip. This liaison continued for nearly a year until Simba was recalled to his family properties and investments in Bhutan.

Sudha, whose ever-active wonky brain was ever scheming, never gave up on her fumbled plans. She had more substantial business to accomplish. Besides settling Ponda into the family inheritance and property she worked tirelessly to garner confidence from Brinda and Deena, the two influential spinsters. Sudha strove to do it in subtle ways. Both ladies were ageing and needed a lot of home care and delicate attentions. Sudha would go out of her way to visit them both, Deena close to her and Brinda in Siliguri. She would go there with gifts and then spend the day just chatting away the hours or attending to their pains and ailments. Both ladies were ever so grateful to her for being there for them.

Each time Sudha went to meet these ladies she also spun a story of doom to them, usually the same story so that it would be believable. She once told them that landslides might wash away their mountain homes, and so they might need to move away to the plains or elsewhere. Deena found that frightening since she would have to abandon her house. Brinda didn't find it in good taste as she would then have to shelter more members of the family in Siliguri. But Sudha had her targets in sight: the properties of these elderly ladies.

Sudha also got close to Biru and Balti. Biru as the eldest of the clan was held in high regard. Balti too was quite a respected figure in the local area, and had acquired a name as a teacher in spite of her ventures not being successful. Biru was the more pious type and got on to church work, starting off a venture that had a social agenda with religious undertones. He was a Bible reader for the attendees of his church sect and so had developed a bit of a reputation as a church leader. Sudha knew she had to win the support of these two elders to support her own plans.

However Biru was not particularly aware of or sensitive to the basic needs of people or to the realities of the geo-political situation. This hill zone was an area that was part of Bengal and yet was in constant turmoil because of the vested interests of certain political groups in the hill region fighting for their rights and privileges. This only left the common man struggling to fend off hunger and family necessities. Biru could never really address these needs of the people in his many hours of preaching or church work. He was reasonably comfortable in his position, not really feeling deprived in any way. Preaching to his church attendees was an academic performance, almost totally unaware of their deprived conditions.

Biru's take on the situation that prayer would solve socio-political issues and that the church was a driving force for peace and development was more a cry than a reality. Half of his regular Sunday attendees were members of his extended family or his rather restricted group of friends. It would appear that Biru got most of his funds from some USA or UK Christian agency or a splinter church abroad, possibly in a European country, that constantly look to fund newer versions of Christianity constantly springing up around the world. These funds, it would appear, seemed to bolster him more than the clientele he was catering to.

When it came to finance to support his lifestyle and his projects, Biru also turned to his younger brother, Billu, whose own approach to society, finance and development always was a bit airy-fairy. When put to the test Billu's one-eyed-giant involvement in the several little projects he achieved as a contractor was restricted to a few small road building or bridge building projects. So, in practical terms the Singh bandwagon was still in the rugged terrains of a typical western movie, firing shots at random or achieving limited objectives. Publicity is what mattered, and that sector was reasonably well promoted and tirelessly too, even if it was to a rather limited audience.

Balti was perhaps the driving force behind Biru, but she had her own ambitious yet unrealistic aims. Her teaching abilities showed a more managerial than supportive role, and her failure to make her school set-up plans succeed, on two occasions, was proof of the pudding. A good looker, she used this charm and a convincing style of speaking to make her projects believable to the naïve audiences around her. Yet some of the skeptical ones had lingering doubts about the possibilities of the theories or schemes. Biru and Balti who were aware that people trusted them as seniors of the area then felt emboldened, to take up a venture that proved to be a scam, the VisaRef ®(VR) scheme. For a while it had engulfed an entire region in south-east Asia. Parts of India had also been affected by it, and soon this hill region also took a beating especially after Balti became its driving force.

There was proof of at least one family in Kurseong, for example, who had invested their entire life's savings in the plan. When VisaRef crashed the man was left with no other option but to commit suicide by jumping off a cliff, leaving a family with 2 children already in debt into further shock and deprivation. There were similar details of other families who were left in distress or where misunderstandings were caused between husbands and wives. Biru and Balti were the chief instruments responsible for this dodgy sale to around 100 families, where some of them had invested amounts between Rs.50,000 and Rs.300,000. More smooth-tongued than Biru as chief promoter of this fast-buck scheme was none other than Balti.

VR had the typical percentage tag on it so apparently the more you invested the more you gained. In reality people who began investing found no returns coming in, which probably meant that the 'chain' had been broken at some point, and so the original group that jumped in headlong perhaps got some gains, but the later investors got stumped. In plain language the scheme was a disaster, and some of the investors lost their entire savings. In their efforts to avoid a nervous breakdown, with investors hounding the couple, Balti and Biru literally had to move residences nearly every month so that a lynch mob (however dreadful this may sound) did not pursue them to a tragic end!

Chapter 9

One-Horse Town

It is difficult to find out where people in this hill area get their cash flow from. The Darshu and Sita story is probably the tip of the iceberg. One has to be watchful of people who dress smartly or talk sweetly. Nearly everyone who is someone claims status and drops by for a chat and a bit of subtle trickery. Many people, especially the women folk, would win top marks for presentation, and fashion too perhaps. But where does the revenue come from? Most people only seem to be doing window shopping and only the shops that sell vegetables, fruits, milk, bread and other personal and household necessities do any realistic sale most days. The rest of the market is a sort of permanent fashion show set up along that one-and-only shopping-highway, the Hill-Cart Road, with the narrow-gauge railway tracks alongside, in this sort of one-horse town.

It would seem that quite a lot of folk want to make a fast buck with little or no effort. Many young people, quite like Darshu, also know how to pass on tiny packs of drugs even while holding on for a longish handshake. The police and the authorities do not have reliable and factual evidence to arrest any of them, and the common man is no wiser that anything untoward is happening. The schools and colleges, it would appear, do not also have a realistic grasp of the situation, and would perhaps be powerless to know where to start to control this growing abuse. Yet the authorities owe it to the common person that a drug-awareness program needs to be promoted in this part of the world.

On another occasion, during the Bhaat Khawai festivities, the couple –Nilesh and Saima- wanted to do a quick trip to Siliguri to do some of their personal shopping, as Kurseong literally has nothing worth on offer. But folks in Kurseong are always looking for opportunities to take advantage of any situation that offers some convenience or promise. The moment a trip is announced there are a host of takers. As soon as the couple accidentally leaked out this information of a proposed trip, Deena was informed. It must have been Sudha who had passed on the information, as she had to arrange for a vehicle for the trip.

In fact, soon after the couple was up that morning Deena was already there. And before they'd finished their breakfast Billu appeared there too, dressed and ready to go. Neither he nor Deena had really informed the couple they intended going on this trip with them. There was nothing the couple could do at this late stage. Actually, it was all about getting a free ride to and back from Siliguri. That apparently was one of the usual ways of 'saving' a buck in this one-track railway town!

The savings made were not only on the travel arrangement and the fare, the entire expenses of the trip, the food, the stop-over at any hotel or other refreshments along the way: all became the responsibility of the one who arranged the trip –our Bhaat Khawai couple! So, from a trip budgeted to cost around Rs. 2000 (£25 or $45) at the most it soon became nearly Rs.4000 because the two seniors had tagged along. That was not all. When Saima wanted to buy a little trinket at the Mall, Deena too was there picking up something for herself. So, who took care of that bill? In Himalayan ways it would have looked rude not to have offered to pay for Deena's items as well. In the end the trip expenses trebled to nearly Rs.6000, quite a bomb for anyone living in the hills.

Actually Billu's tagging on was for other reasons as well. There always was a lot of speculation going on in the family, especially between Billu and Sudha. The two of them were up early every morning. Their first cup of tea was at around 5.00 am, just when most 'night-birds' are enjoying 'beauty sleep', their last dream or their last conjugal bash! That early hour summit meeting of the two lead characters in the Singh clan was clearly an important take off point for many of the schemes of Sudha, when she had to pick on Billu's brains for her plans, or to take advice on nitty-gritty snags that could be affecting her scheming. After all, our Ms Illiterate was cautious enough not to bungle the 'numeracy' part of her fumbling transactions!

The clan also does own quite a few houses in Kurseong. The main home is the one built by Billu's father, up the mountain-side: the house built largely with funds sent by Brinda, for their parents, which Deena occupied. They called it Family House, where they'd sit in meetings to discuss family matters. Then there was the part-hostel one run of Lynda, and finally the house of Biru and Balti a little below the railway tracks. Billu later built his own house, which was somewhat higher up the mountain. All these houses are only about a 5-minute drive from Kurseong railway station.

Sudha saw herself as finally owning all these buildings, at some point in time, but right then for her Brinda's house in Siliguri was the focal point. Brinda was discussing the sale of her house in Siliguri, as it was in her name. She wanted to make arrangements to hand it over. Brinda had already had a good offer, but Sudha had her eye on it, and wanted to know what was happening.

Dinesh and his wife Laila were interested in the house especially since Brinda had already offered to gift the house to Bob, their little son. This is what really disturbed Sudha's wily planning. Brinda was at a point of making the arrangements of the offer, all 'pukka'® as they say, and to get the final seal of approval done as an official 'deed'.

But Sudha did not know at what point the negotiations had reached. So that was why Sudha literally pushed Billu into going on the trip to Siliguri just to pick up any talk of house sale by Brinda. In other words the sale offer from Dinesh had literally thrown the cat among the pigeons. Billu in true lapdog fashion just had to do Sudha's bidding.

Chapter 10
The Hill Connections

Chula was forced into a divorce of which she didn't know very much, because no official papers were given to her. She moved on to stay with a guy called Tombu, possibly of Assamese origin. Tombu who couldn't remember much about his past had been left abandoned in a little village in north Assam, when only a child. A railway porter took pity on him and brought him up. Later, when he was about 10, a wandering group of merchants, travelling by train, had picked him up as their additional porter and had taken him along, and had then left him off at a vegetable seller's in Guwahati, Assam's capital city. Tombu was smart and he seems to have coped well with his vegetable seller, and was after a few years able to set up his own little shop, and then move on.

We know that some years later, he married a tribal Assamese girl, and had 3 children, a girl and a boy. He must have done well because he appears to have lived a fairly comfortable life. But in this semi-matriarchal set-up his wife felt she wasn't getting access to all the cash, and so endless quarrels followed. Tombu in a characteristic hasty decision just left Guwahati and travelled to Kurseong, where his married daughter had earlier run away to. These moves are possible in these traditions because in their set-up the man and the woman share the responsibility of looking after the home. So, whatever his family connections were, the family was not put to any terrible hardship. Tombu could not stand this social tradition where he had to share his money as well as the house chores.

It so happened that Chula's mother's house was close to the 'basti' (village) in Kurseong where Tombu and his daughter lived. Quite by accident Chula's mother was friends with the family where Tombu and his daughter were put up. It is possible that Chula first set eyes on Tombu when she must have accompanied her mother to this friend's place.

Assam is one of the important states in India's north east where several tribal groups co-exist in great cultural harmony. The sort of sturdy mountain culture of Assam with its people, its rich forests and its wildlife has some similarity to that of the Darjeeling region. Also, if one is not familiar with how people living in the hill regions of India look, one is not easily able to distinguish between people from the different hill states. People of the different states look quite alike to the casual non-hill person. When Tombu moved to Kurseong no one recognized him as Assamese.

Chula too moved forward slowly at first, cautiously taking her first few steps after the break-up with Billu. Her mother fortunately was around and gently guided her through her trauma. One late evening during one of these visits of her mother to her friend's house, Chula noticed Tombu chatting with the men folk in the house. He too seemed to throw meaningful glances to her. There seemed to have been an instant link-up. She tugged at her mother to stay on longer so she could hear more of Tombu's stories. Tombu too noticed her staring at him. Soon Chula got her mother to arrange a meeting with Tombu when they could have a proper chat.

With Chula single and Tombu in need of companionship it would appear to have been an ideal match. It gave Chula some confidence to have a man around, but she did not seem to be serious about any permanent arrangement. She felt comfortable with the companionship, with neither of them moving towards getting married, though they must certainly have been more than a platonic couple. Chula looked cared for in every way, and in public they seemed very much in love. Moreover no one questioned such living together in the hills. The hill solutions took care of it all, just letting people live their lives happily. So literally all's well that looks well!

However, even after all the years that had passed, Chula still believed that she could get back to Billu, and so just stopped short of officially marrying

Tombu. She still harboured that pretty naive belief that one day in the future all would be well and hunky-dory, and that she would be re-united to Billu, because she still loved him dearly. She could not accept the fact that Billu was moving away from his family and from her to get the affections of a teenage orphan.

In Kurseong most men work in other parts of India in order to provide for their families. There are very few opportunities in that hill area. So, most homes have single girls and women at home, seemingly ready on offer to wandering men like Tombu. Chula though felt happy with her choice as she got to know Tombu better. Their relationship blossomed though both of them kept some of their skeletons carefully hidden away in secretive cupboards. Tombu had secrets he was too scared to reveal while Chula still entertained banana-skin hopes of meeting up again with her beloved Billu. Meanwhile Chula was just about smart enough to maintain her rather steamy feminine bond with her hunky partner, waiting for developments to take place around her, before she could really move on.

When Billu's mother passed away in the mid 1980s, Laila was just 12 and Saima only 10. Billu's father passed away before his mother, possibly in the early 1980s. Billu was then studying civil engineering in a Darjeeling college, after which he got a Government job, it would seem in the BDO's® office. As business improved he soon began to support Biru with his Christian social work in the Darjeeling-Kurseong region, trying to front an NGO[®] status in what they tried to do. It would appear that they were able to complete some minor construction projects like building roads and small bridges in the Darjeeling and Siliguri areas. However it all got disproportionate publicity as massive NGO projects, because it promoted Biru's church attendance and enhanced Billu's business image. It would appear that during this period at some point in the late 1970s, Billu met Chula who was studying in a Kurseong school, when Chula was 18 and Billu was 24.

Meanwhile, in Kurseong, Billu went ahead with his own plans not quite sure if these were dictated by Sudha or by his own egoistic self-promotions. He built a floor above Deena's house, and cast the concrete slab with funds obtained from selling a property he owned close to his house. But there were no funds to continue with the work after the slab. This expansion was somehow still in progress because Shidu in Canada had supported and invested in the house. Brinda too had contributed towards the construction of Deena's house earlier. In practical terms, the ground floor of the house belonged to Shidu, which Billu used for his socio-religious NGO activities.

But really no one was the wiser on how the Singh family was going to sort out the ownership of these building projects later. It was something that the female grandees never analyzed closely. Only Sudha did some back-tracking in her own street-wise thinking. She had her eye on all the properties, but was cautious in not expressing her opinions in public. She was not even sure how Billu would react if she broached the subject. So there was a sort of calm under this brewing storm, i.e. wry smiles that seemed to say, "Let's just get on with living now... We'll see what happens later."

Chapter 11

Himalayan Objectives

Kurseong is a tiny little town of around 80,000 people and news of success or failure does not take long to circulate in spite of most people not being really bothered about reading the local rag or a national broadsheet or getting news off the television or the internet. The television reception is tolerable while linking up through the net is quite a deal. It would seem that most people keep up with world, national and local news on the radio. In fact there is an All India Radio station for the area in Kurseong town, where news and socio-cultural program are regularly broadcast.

However the sort of news that satisfies people is all about family, clan, community and society. Education too enters the circuit and of course politics. There have been political parties and parties, but most families interviewed would appear to have lost faith in the power of politicians to change the stagnating situation in the area.

With only one road, the Pankhabari route, to communicate with the main source of supply, Siliguri, about 40 km away, the strain on families, in Kurseong, to get their necessary provisions and their other needs is huge. To add to their pressures they have to travel to Darjeeling, their administrative headquarters, a 30 km drive along an ageing, unrepaired tarred road. Most families depend on remittances coming in to keep going and when the postal and other services cannot be relied on the situation gets worse.

With some people out for a fast buck, there is always a lot of arm wrestling going on, and scores of nobodies suddenly turn up as 'saviours' with unheard of rescue plans. Quite naturally those who stack up goods or reasonable bank balances seem to wield the most influence and power. There are always quite a few jostling for positions of importance and control, and naturally there are a few naïve people who get short-changed. Balti, more than Biru, was also somewhere on this broad scene, more on the side of the 'haves' than of the 'have-nots', when she came up with the VR scheme.

Sudha had, over nearly 20 years, systematically worked herself into contention not for a political seat in local government, that only wields power momentarily, but for ascendency in society and for control in the Singh family and in the Kurseong area. Sudha, who really rose from humble beginnings and had, in a way, risen through the ranks, had won the respect and the affections of the seniors of the

Singh clan, of Biru, Brinda, Deena, Lynda and then of course the love and admiration of Billu.

Sudha had a natural instinct to manage people and situations. The age difference did not matter. She had used Gonkul earlier, so getting Billu on board her vehicle of discovery for recovery, power, control and prosperity was all about honing her skills. She had made a beginning, and had moved up the social ladder, from no class to near middle class. There was no turning back. There was a long road ahead but she seemed equipped for it. She was not sure of where she was heading, but her confidence was growing, and each day was like a new school day, and each month or situation became a sort of move reaching for the stars.

From no education she was, after trundling along with the ageing Singhs, risen to Graduation level, in nearly full control of all the Singhs, and what is important, of nearly all the financial clout of the leader of the pack, Billu. In fact, she nearly called 'check mate' when she and Billu had their own child, Ponda. It was like setting the seal of authority over the entire clan.

Actually Sudha was at a stage now when she was almost the uncrowned queen of Kurseong. Every taxi driver, merchant, or any body who was anything had to get to know her or to seek her approval, or at least her advice, for their schemes or projects. Initially she used time and the slow processing of minds and opinions in society to come to be recognized as

Billu's wife. The unpleasantness of being the second wife, after Billu had divorced Chula, had died down by now. Even those who might have remembered the past had lost interest in Chula, and had linked up with the larger family of Billu and Sudha, and their four children.

Sudha was now in the fast forward lane: just wanting Ponda to get on with her studies so that she could take over the dynastic base she was building in her hazy scheming. Ponda was coming along but naturally children take time to grow and mature. Ponda was certainly getting to be a fashionable adult and lady, but the signs were that there wasn't too much of her maturing to be a grown-up. But then Sudha too had taken time to learn the ways of society, and of the Singhs. So, she bided her time.

Yet there were some distress signs flashing up on Sudha's dashboard. Her femininity was struck a blow. To begin with, she was told that she would not be able to conceive again. It certainly was a cause for worry that dampened her usual buoyancy. Billu tried to make it up to her with money, gifts and some travel opportunities. What Billu was not aware of was that Sudha was still attractive at 36, gaining ascendency in this Kurseong world of business, trade, and social structures. He was not aware that the freedom he had given to Sudha was getting her to take control of a lot of what was happening to the Singh family.

Sudha was also using the freedom to help release

the female tensions inside her, and to link up with her earlier flames. She was not able to sense that this degenerating flaw within her was making her lose control of parts of her power-base set-up. It was all getting too complicated for her: keeping the family together, maintaining her ties with Billu and still trying to hold on to her steamy relationships. And now, with her health getting in the way Sudha's enthusiasm, if not her physical endurance, began to show signs of wilting.

It was now time, in the 2000 era: a world of the mobile phone and messaging, to launch out on to a bigger stage. Sudha was not only shrewd, she was smart too. The link ups with Gonkul and with Simba showed she could use her charms, and this gave her cause to think and plan more definitive strokes of her power-wielding brush, even though her health wasn't what it had been and even if not everything was going her way. It was some years now that Billu seemed to be a setting sun. She wanted a new rising moon to pick her up and lead on to some symbolic ballet moves that the world would perhaps notice. The scene was getting complicated for her, but she felt it was still manageable.

Sudha had to hurry on with being signatory to all the investments that Billu had, and to getting Ponda on to whatever inheritances that were on offer from the family. Most of the spade work had been done, and she just hoped that other issues would iron themselves out. There wasn't much she could do with ageing Brinda, Deena or even Lynda. To her Biru and Balti weren't really a problem: as the VR scam would keep them low and ineffective. Her problem really was Billu, however weird it sounded. She loved him, but she didn't see him as sharing her throne as Queen of Kurseong.

Her backup plan was her group of followers in Kurseong. They were really the riff-raff of town: drivers, coolies and cleaners: all tough guys –all men with brawn but no brains. She used her charm and almost transformed this army of no-gooders into a team of do-ers, a band of loyalists and a group of surveillance officers. She gave them a name, Society, and status. They became her unofficial bodyguard, her supporters, her cheer leaders, her close confidants in some cases. She set up home parties for them to keep them humoured. The evening party at the Bhaat Khawai for Nilesh and Saima was for this rabble.

She was hoping, against hope, that she could bring Simba back into her life. Those few years of playful romps with him had not only satisfied her desires as a woman, it had shown his brighter and shrewder side. She thought she was now ready for change, for ruling the kingdom, with a new supporting head, a young, energetic and business-wise Simba, one who also satisfied her youthful zest.

She suddenly took a new interest in training certain members of the Society. They had to track down on movements of Biru, Brinda and Deena, and even Billu, and report to her at regular intervals. All the while she was also aware that the two daughters of Billu married outside the established Nepali settings could prove a danger. So, she kept up a relentless chain of communication with them, and even came to help the second daughter, Saima, after her delivery, even though she knew Saima didn't really like her. She made it a point to take a series of snaps of herself with the baby, to be able to prove to Billu and the rest of the seniors in the clan that she was genuinely taking care of the family at all levels.

As for attending to Laila she found ways to load her with gifts or favours whenever Laila and Dinesh visited India. She hadn't finished off Caesar® (Billu) yet, but she moved tirelessly on the Brutus-plan® to establish a new 'Rome', a new dynasty, in Kurseong! So, how did Kurseong's 'Jhansi ki Rani'® (who faced up to the wily British), or perhaps 'Hitler Didi'® (who learnt to cope with life and emotions in the TV serial), work out her own destiny?

Chapter 12

Himalayan Disaster

On one of his regular trips to Kolkata Billu left in a bit of a hurry. He didn't seem to want to do his usual goodbyes, and actually forgot a few items he usually took on tour like his favourite shirts and his casual wear. The Kurseong female grandees were a bit worried about the hurried trip. Actually Billu's trip came up when Sudha was out visiting Bindya in college in Siliguri. She had gone there to try and convince Bindya to give up her studies only to find out that Bindya was becoming the star student at college.

News about Bindya's successes had already reached Brinda in Siliguri who promptly communicated it to Deena and Lynda. That exposed some of the dodgy stories of Sudha earlier that Bindya was wasting her time studying and that she wasn't capable of academic work. Sudha had become a little unsettled and was feverishly brain-storming her rather depleted brain power on how to steer her wayward plans. Her indifferent health had begun to take a bit of its toll. She was worried that the three grandees would interfere and question her efforts to stop Bindya's progress at college.

Partly frustrated at her failure to convince Bindya to give up her studies, she returned to Kurseong only to more unpleasant news. It wasn't about the female grandees questioning her about Bindya. Billu's plane to Kolkata had run into bad weather and had crashed somewhere on the Bangladesh-Bengal border, in the late afternoon. The sturdy passenger plane, an old Dakota, was on a routine flight when it met disaster leaving everyone in shock. Only 8 of the 20 passengers survived, but 2 of these survivors seemed to have just disappeared. Sudha couldn't get any news of Billu, but believed strongly that he was one of the two unidentified survivors and was alive. The search went on, but Billu did not show up nor were the airline authorities able to throw any light on who the two possible survivors could be.

The initial press and radio reports did not give a clear picture of what had happened. The airline manifest could not clearly identify the survivors, but the six who did survive claimed that they had, in the dusky light, seen 2 people thrown into the rice fields, about a kilometer away, in what was Bangladesh territory. Neither ambulance services nor news-starved journalists could provide any more clues.

The two governments, India and Bangladesh,

were still using their communication systems to try and search for the survivors, if any. The difficult terrain, the rains and the lack of equipment hindered the search. The Indian army helicopters finally did manage to do several sorties and could not spot any survivors. But even this was possibly done too late, i.e. nearly 5 hours after the crash. With fading light and in difficult weather conditions it was quite impossible to continue any realistic search, so the search had to be called off.

Sudha did not know how to react. Billu had always been dear to her, but she had begun to grow cold towards him. So his disappearance seemed like a secret prayer answered. As for Ponda, she didn't quite realize the seriousness of the situation. She had this childish hope that her dad would be ok. Outwardly Sudha was putting on an air of worry and deep sorrow, though secretly she seemed to feel that fortune was playing into her hands. When everyone else was deeply concerned about Billu, she seemed to drown it all in tears inside her house. Were they of sorrow or of joy?

Bizarre as it may seem, she locked herself up in her own room and tried desperately to get in touch with Simba, to let him know about the tragic plane crash, to find out what his reaction was, and to renew her interest in him. This time Simba was quite cold and somewhat unconcerned. He happened to be in town, in Kurseong, to check on the re-development of the lodge and to take a look at future business interests. His replacement was already functioning effectively and only just needed a bit of mentoring. What was even more shocking to Sudha was that he told her over the phone that he wouldn't have time to meet up with her. This cut her up immensely. She seemed to see her house of cards crumbling. Or was she having a bad dream?

Back to reality again, Sudha also had to cope with more urgent attentions. Deena, one of the elders in the clan, suddenly got bed-ridden with varicose veins and acute arthritis. Even though she needed special care those around her weren't really doing much for her. Sudha knew she would have to prove what she always proclaimed, that she would give her life for the family. She had hardly got Deena properly attended to when, down in Siliguri, Brinda had a partial stroke. Sudha had barely reached Siliguri to attend to Brinda when back in Kurseong Lynda took ill with an extremely harmful virus, with a complication of pneumonia and colitis. Her two adopted children, Darshu and Sita, and their partners, did very little even to get the doctors to her. Sita initially helped with nursing her mum, but then she and her partner got very involved in their own chores. Darshu of course, true to form, just didn't lift a finger to support or look after his mum.

It was becoming a bit too much for Sudha with no definite news of Billu too. Sudha mobilized her Society's trusted lieutenants to find out more about the plane crash. But they were generally illiterate for the most part and usually quite un-diplomatic in their dealings. All they gave her was unconfirmed and unreliable reports, given in a disorganized way. This only added to the confusion of Sudha. Even those she might have referred to for advice –Brinda, Deena or Lynda were not around to support her. Her precious darling, Ponda, was really of no use to her just then. In fact, if anything she was becoming a pain, asking for more money to buy some odd trinket or a new more up-to-date mobile phone when everyone else was in shock or terribly worried about Billu.

What was worse was that even Biru and Balti, who at the best of times offered lip service in support of some of Sudha's plans, were not around this time. They had gone off to Kolkata before Billu's trip, to make arrangements for their own future. They were taking a trial run of staying in an old people's home in Kidderpore, in Kolkata. They were planning to use the bits of savings they had made from the VR scheme to fund their retirement there. They were not fully aware of the plane crash of Billu, and of his disappearance since it had happened. Biru and Balti were in their own purgatory: suffering mentally and physically. Their health was a matter of concern to the grandees in the clan, the three sisters. Both were in their late seventies, and they really were badly in need of care and support themselves.

Sudha's dreams of a new 'Rome', a new dynasty in Kurseong, seemed to have come to a crashing halt. Yet she felt hopeful. Though Ponda had failed her degree, she was able to get a Management qualification, via the 'hill method', and had begun to try to pick up the pieces. She didn't seem too concerned about her father missing, though, tutored by Sudha, she kept telling people through her crocodile tears that she really missed her dad. She had latched on to the teenage wing of the Society her mother had set up. One of the showy teenagers who played the guitar had nearly swept her off her feet. She was infatuated and completely drawn into his games, and of course he took full advantage of the situation, with her mother too preoccupied with family issues. He soon got her pregnant before she could even realize what was happening.

Ponda while trying to cope with a teenage pregnancy was also attempting to boss over the people around her and trying to help out in the business interests which her mother was planning to take over. It was too much for the young shoulders of Ponda. She became irritable, erratic and arrogant. Though she gave birth to a healthy baby boy, she had almost totally lost control of her temper. She became the scourge of the place, issuing wild orders and treating her elders, Sudha's clients and Bindya too quite rudely.

It had all become quite unmanageable for mother and daughter, and soon it got much worse. Sudha was diagnosed with ovarian cancer. She had to be rushed to a Kolkata clinic, with Ponda totally confused and really incapable of any decision. It was almost like Mohamed Bin Tugluq® ruling India (with his crazy reforms), or Nero® playing the lyre (while Rome was burning).

Ponda's two married sisters, Laila and Saima, got news of all that was happening, especially the crazy behavior of Ponda. They were shocked about Sudha's condition but were really more worried about their father. They kept a constant search on TV, on Radio, on Facebook® and on Twitter®, but with no luck. They were not sure about how to react to it all, though Saima did convince Nilesh to travel all the way from Goa to Kolkata to check on how Sudha's treatment in hospital was going.

Chapter 13
Himalayan Solutions

Earlier, in spite of all her coaxing, Simba did not want to link up with Sudha. He had become the chief of his tribe, in Bhutan, and had married a local girl of his choice. Moreover now cancer-stricken Sudha began to realize that she didn't stand a chance with Simba. Was that the end of her plans? The three elders, the influential females of the clan, Brinda, Deena and Lynda, who had begun to be suspicious of Sudha's behavior, had all become too ill or too ineffective to oppose her or to control her in any way. The most influential of the lot, Biru and Balti, who had moved out of the scene, almost victims of their own undoing, had picked up rumors of Sudha's dodgy plans and were in no mood to sympathize in spite of Billu's disappearance. In fact all the grandees, still in a state of shock, didn't know how to bring closure to the painful Billu episode.

There was more to come. Laila and Saima, though far away from the scene of the action, had their own sources of information and both, independently, had got eager for the control of some the properties that were rightfully theirs. The two families got in touch with each other by phone but were not too sure of what could be done. Both were deeply involved with their own lives, Laila in her Dubai hospital and Saima in her husband's business. Yet they felt they had to confront Sudha and get their own rightful share of what was due to them.

Sudha in her hospital bed in Kolkata, now a broken woman, could see her kingdom crumbling around her. She was very much like Cleopatra® when she was told that Mark Anthony® had lost his ships, and that they had lost (the battle they had teamed up to fight for and) the control of Rome. The doctor's report said that Sudha was in remission, but that she would not really last another year, as the cancer would recur, with a vengeance.

Ponda, her beloved, was close to despair. Her teenage world had already been partly shattered with her unwanted teenage pregnancy and then the arrival of the baby boy she had to care for and bring up. Surprisingly not even the tender eyes of the little baby, even as he grew up, could brighten Ponda's spirits. Sudha too couldn't see any future for herself or for her daughter, though the little baby was an assurance of the dynasty's continuance –but not as planned by her.

The 3 sons of Biru and Balti were popular around, but had no base, no expertise, and no money to throw around. They gradually took over the clan's assets: Vinak, took over as Director of the Society, Andul got the care of Deena's property, Prakar was given the management of Lynda's sinking business. With Sudha not around the Society took matters into their hands, and a type of gang culture set in. The Society took on a leading role, and presented their teenage heroine, Ponda, as the banner for their exploits. They flouted the law, and local authorities were not really able to control the anarchy caused by the Society. Kurseong indeed was in deep turmoil.

Sudha was given a brief respite from her cancer treatment in Kolkata and she insisted on getting back to Kurseong to see if she could stem the tide of disorder there. However, the Society had gone a bit beyond the point of return. Her own daughter, Ponda, was just drawn into the turmoil because her partner, to whom she was still not married, kept urging her on to stay the course –for complete control of Kurseong, whatever the stakes. Soon the Queen-to-be of the new-Kurseong, the *Boadicea-*model, Sudha, had lost it all –the power base she had built up- her 'Iceni'-tribe, the Society. Most of its members of were rounded up and imprisoned with minimum 5-year sentences. Ponda too was under house arrest for several months, and was allowed out for a few hours at a time to see her mother in the sanatorium.

Laila and Saima decided to step out into clearer waters: into the settings they had built up on their own. They opted to move back to their own greener pastures, and to step away from Ponda and her clan, actually their own folks. Billu was never found, though everything pointed to the fact that he had probably survived the crash. By the end of 2010 the three sisters, elders of the clan, Brinda, Deena and Lynda were fighting for survival of their lives in different medical institutions. Biru and Balti now in an extremely feeble condition, thought it best not to return to the Kurseong area. Their three sons somehow kept hold of the Singh properties, but that really marked the beginning of the end of the Singhs in Kurseong. Or was there yet another surprise in store?

Ponda had really been the surprise package all along. Her two elder married step-sisters seemed to drift away from her, as they found her difficult to deal with. But with the passage of time the memory of the warmth of the family when she was younger had gradually awakened the gentler feelings inside Ponda. There had also been a special meeting up with her mother, Sudha, before she passed away that the rest of the family hadn't really got news of.

In the middle of all the sorting out that Sudha tried to do with her club, the Society, and the authorities, and before the law could clamp down on Ponda because of her involvement with the group, Sudha was able to get some tender moments with her daughter in the sanatorium where she was recuperating. This meeting took place only days before Sudha sadly passed away.

"How are you today, mum?" asked Ponda during this visit.

"Not too well, my dear," Sudha replied. "But I want to tell you something: something very important. I want you to share it with your sisters later, but not just now."

"What's bothering you now, mum?...Don't worry about anything now. Just get well."

"No, I have to tell you. ....Just listen," Sudha insisted.

"OK mum. I'm listening."

"There are many things I did that I realize only now that I should not have done....," Sudha began.

"Now, now, mum, there's nothing wrong you've done...only good...to all the family," said Ponda.

"No, no," Sudha insisted. "Everything may have looked good, but really I was only thinking of you, and forgot everything else. In a way, I must also admit I didn't even think of your Dad, my dearest Billu..."

"I can't believe what I'm hearing," said Ponda.

"But, it's the truth," said Sudha as she went into a spell of coughing. "It's the truth....I don't know why I did it, and I know I can't really forgive myself now...I think I went off the rails a bit."

Soon the nurse had to be called, as Sudha was in tears, and gasping for breath. When she had been attended to, and had rested a while, she continued,

"I liked everyone, and wanted to look after everyone, but I really only felt close to you. You are my dearest daughter. You are part of me.....you are my beloved, in a way even more than my husband."

Soon Ponda was in tears, and the two were hugging each other. Ponda couldn't help but respond, but only when the sobbing had stopped.

"Mum, I know you loved me very much, and still do....I want you to get well, and now I want to look after you. You deserve the best."

"Maybe I do, and maybe that is what I had planned for.... for you and for me, but.... some of the reasons why I did things .....is troubling me now...."

"Like what, mum?" asked Ponda.

"I loved all your aunts, Brinda, Deena and Lynda, and cared for them a lot, but really only in the early years, but....but...as time went on," she began to choke, and had another spell of coughing.

"What happened, then, mum?" Ponda was eager to know.

"As time went on...I did not always look after them because they were really dear to me...... though in the beginning I may have felt close to them," Sudha explained.

"Then why, mum?" Ponda asked again, a little worried now.

"I did it because I wanted them to think well of you," said Sudha." I did it all .... because I wanted you and me to be well provided for, and hoped that they would give you everything.....and then we.... you and I ....could enjoy a long life together...I wanted them to give.... everything....."

"What did you want them to give, mum?" asked Ponda, now getting a little impatient.

"If I hadn't behaved that way you would not have got all the properties, all the inheritances in your name," said Sudha. "I even bullied your sister, Bindya....I was jealous because in spite of her strange behavior she was beautiful, really beautiful and.... your father would have given her everything. He loved her so much... Naturally I was jealous... She was good really, even if a bit crazy...But I wanted everything for you...Bindya and your two other sisters would one day have taken away what I had wanted for you.....all along....Even your dad would have sided with them..."

"That cannot be true, mama. I would certainly have got my share of everything. Dada would have made sure of it all," said Ponda not fully taking in the substance of the revelations.

"No, Ponda," said Sudha, "your elder sisters and their husbands were smart. They would have grabbed everything eventually, and you would have been left with little or nothing."

"Was that the right thing to do, mama?" asked Ponda, more than a little concerned now.

"I don't know if I was thinking right but..... at that time.... I felt it was the right thing to do....But, when I am gone......" Sudha's voice was getting faint, and tears were welling up again.

"Now, mama, you're not going anywhere...You'll be well soon.....You will be well...You will be able to sort it all out...You will have to...Dad is not here now....Just rest.....you are too weak to speak....you are not going to go anywhere....you'll be ok......I need you to clear this up with everyone...." said Ponda.

"No, I.....won't last long....I must tell you...Please be strong, for me... Please tell the family...tell the 3 girls, when you meet them....I love them....and want the best for them...I may not have always done that....especially to Bindya....Dad would have wanted the best for everyone....even for you....,"she started again. "Tell the girls....you must," and then started breathing heavily.

"I will, mama," said Ponda. "You rest now...."

"Tell them ......but only when I am gone.....that if I have deprived them of anything, I want you, Ponda, to sort it out, and to give them what is just.....," she went on. "I am sorry for what I did....tell them...... .I know I will not live much longer...You must be a good girl..."

"I will, mama," said Ponda. "You don't worry now....You're not going...You'll get well....Anyway, I promise you we won't fight over property or other things....even though at the moment they are not in touch with me....We are not really on talking terms....Some time has passed now, and I too feel that I must meet up with them one day soon, and talk.....I really want to talk to them...I miss them a lot...We had some lovely times together....You kept us all together...I will meet up with them."

"That's good," said Sudha. "That's a good girl....I wanted to hear that from your lips."

There wasn't much time for more, as a few days later Sudha passed away in the sanatorium. That left a huge responsibility on the shoulders of young Ponda. Would she live up to it? In reality could she really be the one to whom the Singh torch had been passed on? Was she to be the catalyst?

Chapter 14
Epilogue

Time has moved on. It is the year 2020: two teenagers, Bob and Lee meet up quite accidentally, while travelling on the little narrow-gauge train that goes up from Siliguri to Kurseong. They had never met before as teenagers. Bob was 19 and Lee was 17. They had jumped off the slow-moving train at Sukhna® station, just 30 km after leaving Siliguri. The train had a longish tea stop here, around 10 am. The two boys decided to check out the railway canteen for a sip of famous Darjeeling tea, or perhaps have a coke. They sort of bumped into each other at the canteen, and while waiting for their prized cup of tea had started off an interesting conversation.

"Hi, I'm Bob...I'm from Dubai," said the older one, "though I'm really from Bangalore just now."

"Hi, I'm Lee...I'm from Goa....I'm going to Kurseong... Are you going to Darjeeling?"

"No," replied Bob. "I'm going to Kurseong as well, with my parents, who're here with me."

"That's interesting," said Lee. "My mum and dad are here too."

"So, why Kurseong?" asked Bob.

They soon discovered they had the same surname, Sincruz. Two DeCruz boys had both married Singh girls. Both boys decided, after they had got married, to change their surnames to Sincruz, to make both surnames blend. For official purposes the two boys had kept to DeCruz while the two girls stayed on with Singh, just to help to keep all their legal documents in place. The years had passed and with their own circles of friends increasing they hadn't really kept in touch.

"So, you too are a Sincruz," said Bob. "So who are your parents?"

It didn't take time to find out that both families: i.e. Dinesh and Laila, and Nilesh and Saima, were related and were on the train, in different compartments. For a variety of reasons the two families hadn't really been communicating with each other, so they hadn't planned to do the trip together. For some unknown reason too they hadn't got on to Facebook or Twitter. They hadn't used Emails either to keep in touch. The few phone calls they had made to each other were more about property matters than family relationships. The occasional letter was the only link they had used. So they didn't really know they had chosen the same day to travel and were then on the same train to Kurseong. They were also travelling for the same purpose, to see if they had any claims to the Singh properties and inheritances which were rightfully theirs.

In fact, unknown to them, it was Ponda who had got her lawyers to send both families a written invitation to visit so that they could establish their rights. The request to the two families to visit looked more official than personal and didn't seem to have come from Ponda. Moreover since there had not been any time limit put, they had taken their time to respond and to visit.

The female grandees, Brinda, Deena and Lynda had all gone off, the way of all flesh, and so had Biru and Balti. Billu was never found, and cancer had eventually got the better of Sudha. But the three sons of Biru and Balti: Vinak, Andul and Prakar, who had put up some initial resistance to the arrangements finally agreed to all the legal decisions. The courts settled for Brinda's properties going to Dinesh, Deena's property going to Nilesh. Vinak decided to step away as the Society too had been disbanded by the Police. He chose to keep to the school he owned. Andul and Prakar got the property of Lynda, which they decided to share. Darshu had crossed all limits and had to be taken care of by the State's 'correction squads', while Sita and her partner found it wiser to move down to a new little home in Siliguri, where Sita took up sewing. Kurseong was quite a normal place again. Time had moved on for Ponda too, who inherited the ancestral home of Billu.

Taking up the invitation of the lawyer, the two daughters of Chula decided, quite independently really, to use the occasion to meet up with Ponda for a possible reconciliation. They didn't realize that it would turn out to be quite the surprise it turned out to be. Perhaps it was something they had secretly hoped would happen in their lifetime.

Bindya, whom Ponda's lawyer had also sent a note to, could not visit, as she was busy with her nursing work in Oman, where she had found a wonderful match in a dashing Suleiman. They were happily married and she was doing really well as the Matron at the Ruler's Court. At one point she offered to take Sita and her husband there, as the ladies in court needed a seamstress. Later, when legal issues did come up, and they were able to get in touch with her, she decided not to claim any property or inheritance, as she felt comfortable with her earnings. However, Dinesh and Laila offered her a floor of the three-storey building in Siliguri, which was now theirs, whenever she wanted to visit or to stay for a while.

Apart from the shocking revelations from her mother, which definitely affected her, Ponda, had sobered down quite a bit. Her short experience under house-arrest had also helped smoothen out her brash lifestyle. She had, to put it plainly, come to her senses. Also the child she had, now 15-year-old

Amul, had also brought some sense of achievement into her life. With her mother not there and her father no longer on the scene she knew she had to manage her own affairs. Her fiery lover-partner, in the strange affair at the height of the Society's rule, had also left her. Now, at 30, she was handling her own life, still doing some commercials for radio and TV, reasonably secure financially to handle her affairs. She also took up part-time politics and was elected as a member of the local Panchayat®. There was a strange feeling of togetherness when she saw her sisters come back to see her.

"Hi, everyone....Missed you all," she said, as she hugged them all: Nilesh and Laila, Dinesh and Saima and their children. There was no feeling of bitterness or ill-feeling noticeable.

"Yes, missed you too," said Nilesh and Laila, as they hugged her.

"We too missed you," said Dinesh and Saima.

"I miss mama very much," said Ponda as she burst out crying.

"We're here now," Laila tried to comfort her.

"We're together once again," said Saima. "That's what's important."

"I'm missing Dad too," Ponda spoke through her tears.

"We too miss Dad," Laila and Saima spoke almost in unison.

"But, I want to tell you all a little secret," said Ponda, "something that no one in the family knows."

"What, are you pregnant again?" asked Laila in jest.

"I think she's getting married," said Saima in quite a teasing way.

After a little giggle, "No, not really," said Ponda. "But perhaps the news is good news for us all, I think."

They pulled their chairs closer together and were all ears. "Let's hear it then," said Laila.

It looked like the old days were back again: the girls getting together again for some fun, or some gossip perhaps, with their young husbands listening on. But the look on her face seemed to tell another story. Ponda for once had this expressionless look, one that showed she had poise and maturity. Her eyes looked somber yet confident. Her elder sisters could see that Ponda was not only now the heiress to the family home, but also to a long tradition. They seemed to see Chandni and Ratan, their father Billu, their mother Chula, and even Ponda's mother Sudha all rolled into that mature look as she prepared to make that dramatic pronouncement. Would it have a Facebook or Twitter flavor, or would it be the live moment that even YouTube® would never be able to capture? It was in some ways as grand as those momentous words when Mark Anthony began, "If you have tears, prepare to shed them now!" All credit to Ponda as she began,

"Before she passed away, in the sanatorium, mama told me a few things that you perhaps don't know. She really didn't have time to speak to you all....You'll have to believe me for this....It is serious stuff, and our three boys don't really need to hear all this adult stuff...at least not just right now...."

"They could go for a walk up the hillside or get on to the computer or watch television," Nilesh suggested.

"Or just chill out together, in the garden," Dinesh offered. "I'm sure they'll enjoy that."

"Sounds good," Saima and Laila said in unison.

When the three boys had left the room, Ponda once again took on this look of pain and joy blending into one solemn stance as she spoke. Ponda recalled the entire episode where Sudha had made those revelations about her behavior and about her partiality towards Ponda. She also told them about how she now wanted Ponda and the other girls to stay united, and to share equally whatever there was to be shared.

"That's astounding," said Laila. "We really missed listening to your mum saying it all herself."

"Fascinating stuff," Saima agreed. "How refreshing to hear you tell us all this."

"You've really been brave to have gone through so much," said Nilesh. "Above all, your mama's words and the way you so sweetly explained it all seems to have brought resolution to everything.... All our worries have been put to rest... It's great.. and it's fair."

"It's a good omen indeed that the two of us families decided to come here, Ponda, even though we hadn't planned on being here together...Your story has truly re-enkindled our relationships," said Laila.

"But you've certainly changed, Ponda," Dinesh commented. "You're different now, so mature and so much in control. What did you do to yourself?"

"Well, it's a long story," said Ponda. "But, I guess it's just growing up, though I should add, that time of house-arrest was horrible. Yet, it made me think. I think it helped me come to my senses."

"Was that it then? It changed you?" Nilesh asked.

"Well, yes and no. It was mama's revelations too that helped me realize how far I had wandered from the family, from you all and....," said Ponda as she shed a few more tears.

"It's over now," said Laila, giving her a hug. "It

will all be well soon, believe me."

"I hope so. But I'm still missing Dad so much," said Ponda. "He did so much to keep us together.... He is one person who is the real common link. He's your dad and my dad....Will we ever find him?"

"We too miss him so much," said Saima. "Though the chances of finding him are slim, I think."

"I still feel he may have survived somewhere in Bangladesh, where the plane is supposed to have crashed," said Laila. "But it's a long time now, and it doesn't look like a possibility."

"They would have found him by now, or Dad would have got in touch," said Dinesh. "He may have survived the crash, but then must have perished in those fields as no one could reach him."

"I think we'll just have to live with it....and just pray for his soul," said Nilesh

"Yes, let's remember this meeting up, of which Dad too would have been proud," said Laila.

"Our meeting up now has become such a happy occasion," said Saima. "I feel so good about it,"

"Maybe we need to meet oftener, and keep up our ties. We need to keep our families united... our children and their families...in time to come," Dinesh insisted.

"Why don't we meet up once a year, or once every two years, just to celebrate the good times we have had," said Nilesh.

"Sounds wonderful," said Dinesh. "We need to pass on this flame of love and togetherness, like an Olympic torch to our children...Let's go for a Christmas date to start with."

"Yes, sounds good. Let's forget all the unpleasant happenings of the past, and start afresh," said Laila.

"That would be really nice," Ponda chimed in. "Mama would have been so happy...I wish we could also get Bindya to come along...I haven't seen her too in ages."

"Yes we must get in touch with Bindya," Saima insisted, "and tell her about our meeting."

So, that is how the Singh family got together again, even if not all of them were called Singhs in the end. The younger Singhs were definitely on different wave lengths, more positive and optimistic. Their resilience and their fresher approaches to life were good omens for a new chapter in the Singh Saga.

The End

GLOSSARY & REFERENCES

-**Aishwarya Rai:** One of the most famous female stars of Bollywood® movies.

-**Alexander:** Alexander the Great of Greece: who is still considered to be one of the greatest generals and conquerors who ever lived. His conquered peoples also took on Greek Culture and civilization.

-**Anglican:** A Christian group, founded in England, where the Queen is head of the Church, and where the Archbishop of Canterbury is the church leader for all official and religious purposes. There are around 80 million Anglican followers around the world, and it is the third largest Christian church after the Catholic Church and the Eastern Orthodox Churches.

-**Assam:** One of the larger states in north east India. Area: 78.5 sq.km. Population: 31,170,000

-**Assamese:** a person from Assam.

-**Bagdogra:** The airport closest to Siliguri, Kurseong and Darjeeling.

-**Bangalore:** The capital of the Indian state of Karnataka, has a population of approx 8.5 million. It is also known as the Garden City for its gardens and as the Silicon Valley because of the IT expertise it exports. Situated in the Deccan Plateau it is also quite a central air, railway and road hub for south India.

-**Bangladesh:** with a population of about 145 million it is surrounded by Indian states (Bengal) on the west and (Assam & other states) and Burma on the east, and has the Indian Ocean to its south.

-**BDO:** Block Development Officer: quite a senior Government officer in India.

-**Bengal:** The state of West Bengal, in eastern India. 89,000 sq km. Population: 91,000,000.

-**Bengali:** The language of Bengal and Bangladesh; spoken by approx 300 million people worldwide.

-**Bhaat Khawai:** A traditional Nepali cultural celebration, to mark the eating of the first morsel of food by the baby, at the end of breast-feeding, usually held in the girl's parents' home.

-**Bhutan:** An independent country north-west of India, bordering on China, Nepal, Bangladesh and the Indian States of Sikkim and Bengal. Area: around 38,000 sq km. Population: around 700,000.

-**Bible:** the Holy Book of the Jews and of all Christians (Catholic and others). It is broadly divided into the Old Testament (39 books) most parts generally accepted by most Christian denominations and Jews, and the New Testament (27 books), the purely Christian section. Over 5 billion copies of this book have been sold worldwide. The annual sales of the book are estimated at approx 25 million copies.

-Bihar: One of the more populous states, in eastern India.99,000 sq.km. Population: 104,000,000

-Bishop: A senior priest, who rules a Diocese and is in charge of a number of priests. A Christian term.

-*Boadicea*: The Queen of the Iceni tribe in the London area who put up stiff resistance against the conquering Romans, in 60 AD, who had dishonoured a treaty set up by her father. The Romans suffered heavy losses but eventually overpowered this determined Briton, who fought for her land, and who still remains a symbol of British courage and pride. (also spelt Boudica)

-Bollywood: the largest film producing centre in India, and probably in the world, in Mumbai. Bollywood produces Hindi movies largely, which account for about half the total number of nearly 3000 films a year produced in the different languages in India.

-Brutus: The leading Senator who assassinated Julius Caesar, the Ruler/Emperor of Rome, in 44 BC.

-Caesar: Julius Caesar: the unrivaled leader of the Roman world. He was assassinated by Brutus and a group of Senators, in 44 BC, jealous of his power. Shakespeare's play Julius Caesar made this part of Roman history very popular, especially with the speeches of Mark Anthony and Brutus.

-Catholic: the largest Christian group, with around 2 billion followers worldwide.

-Christian: a follower of Jesus Christ. About 33% of

the world's population is Christian today, or about 2 billion in numbers; half of them are Catholic.

-Christian Brothers: An education Order in the Catholic Church, with schools around the world. It was founded in Ireland. They were also known as the Irish Christian Brothers.

Cleopatra: Ruler of Egypt, was really of Greek origin. Her beauty attracted liaisons with Julius Caesar, and later with Mark Anthony®, who teamed up with her to fight for command of Rome.

-Convent: (convent-school): a place where Nuns live. They often have a school attached to a convent.

-Cupid: In contemporary popular culture, Cupid is shown shooting his bow to inspire romantic love, often as an icon of Valentine's Day. In Roman mythology, Cupid is the god of desire, affection and erotic love. He is often portrayed as the son of the goddess Venus, with a father rarely mentioned. His Greek counterpart is Eros. Cupid is also known in Latin as Amor. The bow and arrow are his symbols.

-Darjeeling: The main town in the Himalayan region, in northern Bengal, which was established by the British as one of their summer camps, while also setting up education centers based on the Public Schools system. (also spelt Darjiling)

-Darjeeling Railway: Built between 1879 and 1881, it is about 86 kilometres (53 mi) long. The elevation level is from about 100 m (328 ft) at New Jalpaiguri (and Siliguri) to about 2,200 metres (7,218 ft) at

Darjeeling. The daily Kurseong-Darjeeling return service and the daily tourist trains from Darjeeling to Ghum (Ghoom) (India's highest railway station) are handled by vintage British-built B Class steam locomotives. Since 1999 the train has been a World Heritage Site as listed by UNESCO. The railway originally ended at Siliguri, but was later extended to New Jalpaiguri to connect to the new broad gauge.

-**David:** who is mentioned in the Book of Kings, in the Bible®, is also said to have composed many of the Psalms in the Bible, and to have recited and sung some of these Psalms publicly, in prayer. David is also the ancestor of the line from which Christ was descended. David is an important Bible character.

-**Dhobi:** The Hindi word for Laundry man.

-**Diocese:** A territory/zone that a Bishop® or Archbishop is in charge of. A term used by Christians.

-**Dubai:** One of the leading trading centres in the Middle East, in the United Arab Emirates (UAE) where many ex-patriate workers from India worked, and where they still form the bulk of the population. Dubai, in the 70s and 80s, proclaimed itself as the epitome of a flourishing city built on sands and wastelands. It has taken the lead in developing a modern infrastructure with exciting tourist attractions. It is also known for its exciting Duty Free shopping, and the Gold Souk.

-**Femme Fatale:** An alluring woman who leads men into dangerous situations by her charm.

-Gangtok: Capital of the Indian state of Sikkim.

-Goa: The state on the west coast of India, a formerly a Portuguese colony, was annexed by India in 1961. Area: 3,702 sq km. Population: 1.5 million. The smallest state in India. Known for its beaches it is also a very popular international tourist destination.

-**Goan:** A person from Goa.

-**Ghum:** One of the little towns on the Silguri to Darjeeling Hill-Cart road, about 5 km before one reaches Darjeeling. It has the famous Buddhist Ghum Monastery, and Tiger Hill, one of the best sunrise viewing points in the world, nearby.(also spelt Ghoom).

-**Gurkha:** A name derived from the saint, Gorakhnath. Gurkhas were from eastern Nepal. They formed part of the British-Indian army, and were also an integral part of the British army in World War II.

-**Guwahati:** The capital of the state of Assam, in India. Population: approx ½ million. It is known for its Hindu temples and for the Indian Institute of Technology.(Formerly known as Gauhati)

-**Highland lass:** A Scottish/British term, used in poetry, for a girl from the hills or a mountainous region.

-**Hill-Cart Road:** The 80 km road route from Siliguri in the plains to Darjeeling in the hills, close to the Himalayan range of mountains.

-**Himalayan:** The region bordering the Himalaya Mountains (Himalayas) north of India, which have some of the tallest snow-capped mountains in the world, including Mount Everest, the world's tallest mountain. The Darjeeling hills are bordering these mountains.

-**Hindi:** One of India's national languages with English, spoken by at least 35% of the population.

-Hitler Didi: One of the popular serials (soaps) on Zee TV channel, broadcast in India. The heroine here, Hitler Didi, seems to have all under her control, but finally shows that she too is vulnerable.

-**Hookah:** also known as Shisha: It is literally flavoured tobacco smoked through a contraption, (the Hookah) a sort of glass receptacle with water through which the tobacco smoke is filtered before it is inhaled. It is quite a popular practice worldwide, especially in India, Pakistan and Persia.

-**Hunger Games, The:** A female-centric story with a Twilight-styled® love triangle that appeals to men and boys. The film, and its two sequels, acts like a mirror of the here and now with its privileged haves and impoverished have-nots and its satiric commentary on random celebrity and the perverse pleasure of viewing the misfortune of others from the comfort of your living room.

-**Iceni Tribe:** See *Boadicea*

-**Israelites:** The older Biblical name for the inhabitants of Israel. They were really the eventual settlers of Judea and Samaria: the Jews and Samaritans of the Bible. In their nomadic period they were the 'children of Israel', the Israelites. Today the term refers to the 'lay' person in the religious hierarchy.

-Jamshedpur: known as the steel city of India, it is in the Jharkhand state, and with 2 ¼ million people is the 3rd most populous city in eastern India. City named after Jamshedji Tata, the great industrialist.

-Jesuits: A teaching Catholic Order, with schools, institutions and programs around the world. The Order works in 115 countries around the world in 6 continents, and has a little over 19,000 followers.

-Kalimpong: (also spelt Kalimpang): a little town south of Gangtok (Sikkim), and east of Darjeeling.

-Katrina Kaif: A model and one of the popular female stars of Indian Film. Born in Hong Kong of a Kashmiri father and a British mother, she's British, and acts in Hindi films. Voted Asia's sexiest woman by 'Eastern Eye' in 2008,2009 & 2010, she also acts in Telegu and Malayalam movies.

-Kilimanjaro: the highest mountain in Tanzania. It's on the border of Tanzania and Kenya in East Africa.

-Kolkata: The capital of the state of Bengal in India. Population: 14 million+. It was India's capital till 1911, and the centre of British colonial activity till the focus shifted to New Delhi. It is a city known for its art, culture, and sport, with the Victoria Memorial and the Howrah Bridge as two of its iconic structures. It was formerly known as Calcutta.

-Kurseong: A town about half-way up on the Siliguri-Darjeeling road link. Population: 80,000.

-Loreto nuns: A catholic Order of nuns that runs schools across the world. It was founded in Ireland.

-Maharashtra: One of the larger states on the west coast of India.

-Mark Anthony: Roman politician and general, a friend of Julius Caesar, who ruled Rome. In the course of his military exploits he supports Cleopatra of Egypt, and then falls in love with her. Their joint armies are defeated by the Roman army led by Octavius Caesar. Mark Anthony's character and his famous speeches in the play Julius Caesar by William Shakespeare have immortalized him.

-Methodist: A Christian group, numbering around 70 million followers. It is the evangelistic revival, started by John Wesley, within Anglicanism, and has believers around the world. The missionary sprit of this church was instrumental in spreading the gospel message across the British Empire. It is sometimes referred to as the Wesleyan movement.

-Mid-Summer Night's Dream, A: One of William Shakespeare's plays.

-Mirik: is about 50 km away either north from Siliguri or from south west from Darjeeling (or from Ghum nearby), and is situated on a plateau-like mountain visible from miles around from the semi-circle of mountains, right from Kurseong to Ghum. Because of its more pleasant climate than either Darjeeling or Kurseong it was once thought of, in recent times, as the alternative town to Darjeeling. It still has plans towards that development. Mirik has a direct access road routes from Ghum or from Siliguri.

-Mohamed bin Tugluq: Idealist ruler of Delhi Sultanate (1325-1351), in Indian History, whose experiments with coinage and with the shifting of the Capital away from Delhi, have made him the butt of jokes, though he was otherwise quite a learned man. During his reign the country fell apart.

-Moses: A towering figure in the Bible®, who led the Israelites (the people of Israel), over 40 years, from captivity to freedom in the Promised Land, which he himself never reached.

-Mumbai: Formerly known as Bombay (renamed in 1996) the most populous city in India, on the west coast, is also the 4th most populous city in the world: Population approx. 20.5 million

-Nagpur: A city in the centre of India, in the state of Maharashtra.

-Nepal: A country on India's northern border has China to its north and India to its south. Of its 27 million people nearly 2 million live out of Nepal, a large number of these in the Darjeeling-Sikkim region.

-Nepali: Spoken by about 30 million people worldwide, mainly in Nepal and in India. Sikkim, West Bengal and Assam are the main states in India where it is spoken. Nepal is where the language originated.

-**Nero:** who ruled Rome from 58 to 64 AD: was probably responsible himself for setting Rome on fire so he could blame the Christians for it, and set the new structures he had in mind for improving Rome. Some stories reported (not verified) that he played the lyre while Rome burned. His full name was Nero Claudius Caesar Augustus Germanicus.

-**NGO:** Non-Governmental Organization: one that supports Government in its broad agenda of social and economic development. It is generally a non-profit organization that operates privately.

-**Nun:** A member of a female Catholic Order, who live in Convents and also run schools do other work for the betterment of society, e.g. orphanages, charitable homes, hospitals [e.g. Mother Teresa's Order].

-**Nymph:** A spirit, like a goddess, believed to inhabit areas of natural beauty such as woods, mountains, rivers, and so exuding beauty and charm. A beautiful woman, offering charming and relief in the story.

-**Order:** Another name for Society, Congregation or Organization in the Catholic Church.

-**Panchayat:** A local unit for Government Administration. There are Village, Block (group of villages) and District Panchayats. There could be 5 or more members, all elected to office usually for a 5-year term.

-**Pankhabari Rd:** The shorter road route from Siliguri to Kurseong and Darjeeling. It is about 30 km shorter than the Hill-Cart road route.

-**Patna:** Capital of the state of Bihar in India.

-**Priyanka Chopra:** One of the popular stars in Hindi films in Bollywood®.

-**Public School:** Schools established in England, where the 'public' fee-paying people, and not just the Aristocracy, could attend special schools, based on an all-round education. Eton is one such example.

> Eton College, founded in 1440, a symbol of British Education, producing 19 British Prime Ministers, is one of 9 Public Schools that had to take in the 'public' outside the Royalty and Aristocracy.

-**Pukka:** A Hindi word used in English, meaning 'complete', 'finally sorted' or even 'a deal'.

-**Raja:** A king or ruler. The British actually took over several kingdoms and their Rajas when they ruled India for a while.

-**Rani of Jhansi:** Lakshmi Bai, the Rani (Queen) of the Maratha-ruled princely state of Jhansi, in India,[1835-1858], was the symbol of Indian resistance to the British, and was a leading figure in the Indian revolt to the British in 1857.

-**Rome:** The capital of Italy. Rome is famous for its ancient Roman civilization that influenced the world.

-Shakespeare: William Shakespeare: English poet and playwright. Julius Caesar and A Midsummer Night's Dream are two of the 37 plays he wrote.

-Sikkim: A small independent state of India, in the north-east, bordering on Darjeeling.

-Sikkimese: A person from Sikkim.

-Siliguri: The second largest town/city in West Bengal, India, at the cross-roads of several states and countries in the north-east of India.

-Soonadah: A little town half-way between Darjeeling and Kurseong, on the Hill-Cart road that goes up from Siliguri in the plains up to Darjeeling in the Himalayan hills. (also spelt Sonada).

-Sukhna: One of the first stations of the train on the Siliguri to Kurseong-Darjeeling route.

-Tanzania: A country in east Africa where Swahili is spoken. The name derives from the union of two former countries: Tanganika and Zanzibar (Tan-Zan-ia). It was a former British Protectorate.

-Theologate: An institution where Catholic Priests trainees do their last 3 or 4 years of training, and where they study Theology.

-Times of India: One of India's dailies, published from more than one point. The Edition of April 3, 2012 (from Goa) is quoted in the story.

-Tsunami: A Japanese term to mean huge tidal waves, larger and more destructive than sea waves, usually restricted to coastal areas. The term is here loosely applied to an engulfing social disaster.

-**TTC:** Teachers' Training College.

-**Twilight movies:** The Twilight Saga: a series of 5 fantasy films based on 4 novels by US author Stephanie Meyer. The first movie was out in 2008. Though the series has caught the imagination of teenagers across the world, with Robert Pattinson (vampire) and Kristen Stewart (human teenager) becoming heartthrobs for millions, the critics' reviews of the films have generally not been very positive.

-**Vestal Virgin:** The Vestal Virgins, who maintained the Sacred Fires in the Roman temples, were an integral part of the Roman/Greek socio-religious culture. They were priestesses who were respected, but they had to dedicate their lives to the temple for at least 30 years, after which they could marry. They were generally primed to respond to important clients, e.g. Alexander the Great, Julius Caesar.

-VisaRef: A financial scheme that went bust soon after it was created and circulated. However it ruined many families right across East Asia who invested large sums in it. The percentage scheme didn't work in the Kurseong area as well, where Biru and Balti ran it.

-**Wikileaks:** An organization founded by an Australian internet activist, Julian Assange, and a website launched in 2006, that exposes secret information. The wikileaks in the story are 'unofficial' sources that the individuals set up or arrange that provide the background or information required.

-YouTube: a video-sharing Web site started in 2005.

Reviewers' Backgrounds

-**Beena Menon:** Beena, who has a doctorate in Management and a Masters in French, and in ESL, was lecturer in English Language and Student Advisor at Chiang Mai Rajabhat University, Thailand. Earlier she was Head of the School of Languages at KIIT University, Bhubaneswar, Orissa, India. Before that she was Head of Languages at Symbiosis International University, Pune, India. Beena was also a Training Consultant for Teacher Education for the British Council in India. She keeps up with the latest trends in socio-educational training and people skills needed for employment and performance.

-**Xavier Pinto:** Xavier has a Commerce degree and majored in Hospitality and Tourism in which he won awards as a Research Consultant from Ryerson University. He was selected as a top expert by the Ontario Hostelry Institute for his work with student researchers. He featured in the Ted Rogers School of Hospitality publication as one of the 'faces of the future', commended for his people skills. Xavier also volunteers as a Medical Escort for disabled people, especially the visually impaired. He used his people skills to coach more than 200 tennis enthusiasts, from toddlers to elders. He reads books on topics ranging from beliefs and suspense to today's trends in technological, commercial and socio-educational issues.

-Fred Gomes: Fred taught English in Queensland, Australia, for over twenty years, after a very successful career of teaching English and Drama at La Martinere, Kolkata, and B.Ed courses in Loyola, Jamshedpur, India. He also keeps up his co-curricular interests especially in teaching Ballroom Dancing for competitions in New Zealand and in Adelaide, Australia, after he first got a Gold Medal himself. Fred's experience in working with people and in evaluating the written work of students in institutions adds credibility to his comments. He still uses his people skills in education projects.

-Joe Thompson: Joe worked for several years doing project work in India and in East Africa. He set up several programmes for school drop-outs and other young people to develop their trade skills. His financial expertise and his knowledge of local settings helped organize training and assessment programs in the region. He has several years of experience as a manager in institutions. Joe is aware of market trends in employment and keeps in touch with business organizations to know of the latest trends in employment and in people management.

-Phil Mathews: Phil has built up a portfolio of successful training ventures at several institutes of adult training in India and abroad. His own rich background in training and assessment, also as a manager, has helped him understand people in their settings and in their needs. His efforts to help young people into employment and to counsel them towards their futures also built up his own expertise in dealing with adults and in project work. He used his motivational skills to set up outreach projects where his people skills helped to achieve successful outcomes.

-Jerry & Bernie Crasto (Husband & Wife): They had successful teaching careers in the United Arab Emirates. Bernie also headed a Primary Department. Now settled in Canada, Bernie continues to support local Council ventures in education and parental counseling, while Jerry offers guidance to secondary students and adults in Language and other academic courses they do. Both continue to deal with people and human development as well as with current issues on society, culture, education and environment.

MAP OF DARJEELING AREA

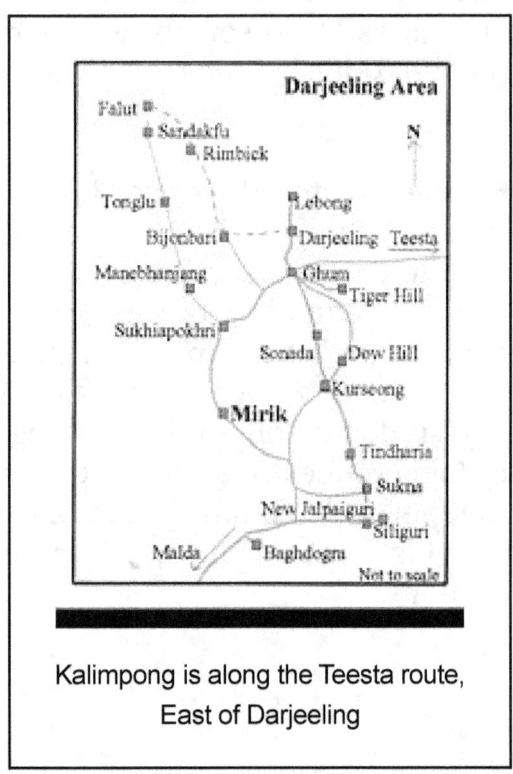

Kalimpong is along the Teesta route,
East of Darjeeling

Map © Wikipedia